"Maybe I should leave," Alex said, her voice full of hurt and confusion.

"Is that what you want?" Damon asked.

The question stopped her. Loving this man was not wise. Danger surrounded him, emanated from him. If she could avoid the danger, she would, but to have the man, she understood she might have to accept the danger. Her grandmother had taught her that the things one regretted most in life were those one hadn't done.

"No." She knew her decision was irreversible. "I don't want to leave." She began to unfasten her dress, offering herself to the man she loved. Damon's need hit him so fiercely he knew he had no choice but to take her precious gift.

When she raised her arms to unwind the pearls from around her neck, Damon stopped her. "No," he said. "Leave the pearls on. . . ."

WHAT ARE *LOVESWEPT* ROMANCES?

They are stories of true romance and touching emotion. We believe those two very important ingredients are constants in our highly sensual and very believable stories in the *LOVESWEPT* line. Our goal is to give you, the reader, stories of consistently high quality that may sometimes make you laugh, sometimes make you cry, but are always fresh and creative and contain many delightful surprises within their pages.

Most romance fans read an enormous number of books. Those they truly love, they keep. Others may be traded with friends and soon forgotten. We hope that each *LOVESWEPT* romance will be a treasure—a "keeper." We will always try to publish

LOVE STORIES YOU'LL NEVER FORGET
BY AUTHORS YOU'LL ALWAYS REMEMBER

The Editors

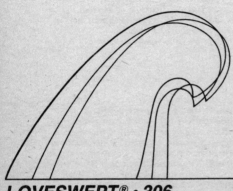

LOVESWEPT® • 306

Fayrene Preston
The Pearls of
Sharah I:
Alexandra's Story

BANTAM BOOKS
TORONTO • NEW YORK • LONDON • SYDNEY • AUCKLAND

THE PEARLS OF SHARAH I:
ALEXANDRA'S STORY

A Bantam Book / February 1989

LOVESWEPT® *and the wave device are registered*
trademarks of Bantam Books, a division of
Bantam Doubleday Dell Publishing Group, Inc.
Registered in U.S. Patent
and Trademark Office and elsewhere.

If you would be interested in receiving protective vinyl
covers for your Loveswept books, please write to this address
for information:

Loveswept
Bantam Books
P.O. Box 985
Hicksville, NY 11802

ISBN 0-553-21957-X

Published simultaneously in the United States and Canada

Bantam Books are published by Bantam Books, a division
of Bantam Doubleday Dell Publishing Group, Inc. Its trade-
mark, consisting of the words "Bantam Books" and the
portrayal of a rooster, is Registered in U.S. Patent and
Trademark Office and in other countries. Marca Registrada.
Bantam Books, 666 Fifth Avenue, New York, New York 10103.

PRINTED IN THE UNITED STATES OF AMERICA

O   0 9 8 7 6 5 4 3 2 1

The Pearls of Sharah Series
is dedicated with all my love
to my sons,

Greg and Jeff,

two very special people.

Prologue

Persepolis
515 B.C.

Far beneath the surface of the swelling waves, in the dark, mysterious, primordial depths of the sea, the pearls grew and waited.

Until . . .

King Darius was coming.

Princess Sharah sat by a pool of still water while a handmaiden ran a comb through the shimmering length of her black hair. Lotus blossoms floated on the pool that reflected the princess's serenely beautiful face. But just as the water hid the dark roots of the blossoms, so, too, did her serene countenance hide troubled thoughts.

With a wave she dismissed the handmaiden. None of the servants had yet sensed their lord's approach, but Sharah did not need to see him or even to hear the soft tread of his footsteps to know he was near. She did not require Darius's presence to feel his every breath. She could not explain why this was, nor did she need to. She was a princess of the Karzana, a nomadic tribe, and she accepted that there were powers which could not be understood.

All she needed to know was that her blood sang when he strode through the halls of the great palace toward her private rooms here in the tower, and that the very air around her seemed to fill with excitement.

There was a stirring among her handmaidens. One of them tittered, then another. Ah, now they also knew he was coming.

Darius was drawing close.

On those nights when Darius came to her bed-chamber, she accepted his attentions because circumstances had forced her to do so. She also writhed in pleasure beneath him, because he was a lover of great accomplishment. And afterward she held him through the night until dawn, because secreted within her heart was a profound love for him.

But she was also proud, and she refused to surrender her soul to him as he was determined she would. . . .

With the power of a great wind, Darius strode

into the chamber and clapped his hands. "Leave us."

The serving girls bowed and dispersed.

Sharah lifted her head and gazed at him. Every line of his strong body bespoke command and power. Even without the royal robes he wore he would have looked kingly. Nevertheless, his *candy* was of bluish-purple; his sash was of cloth of gold; and his shawl was ornamented with rubies, emeralds, sapphires, and diamonds.

The gods had bestowed all the manly graces on Darius, Sharah thought once again, and she knew that hearts beat fast within the breasts of all the fair young women upon whom he deigned to look.

But it was only she he wanted. And so she waited.

He held out his hand to her. "Come here, my love."

The dark blue silk of her full trousers and tunic murmured as she rose and moved with unconscious grace toward him. "My lord?"

He cupped his fingers around her chin and lifted her face to his. "Five years, Sharah. Why do you still insist upon calling me 'my lord' when we're alone? I've asked you not to."

She cast her eyes downward. "You are King Darius, ruler of all Persia. I am your concubine."

He stifled his impatience. "You are my beloved."

"I am your property, taken from my people as you swept through my country in your quest to expand your empire."

"How could I have left you?" he whispered

roughly. "One look at that beautiful face of yours and my heart was lost."

Her dark eyes flashed fire at him. "Yet you keep me prisoner."

"Prisoner, Sharah? Gaze around you. What do you see? This is not a prison. This is one of the finest rooms in the palace." In anger and frustration he jerked the miter from his head and hurled it across the room. "No, I am *your* prisoner."

Darius's temper was legendary, and his action would be guaranteed to send brave men scurrying for cover.

Sharah simply met his hard gaze with a soft question. "Then I'm free to leave?"

"You know I cannot allow that. I cannot live without you. I will not."

She smiled sadly and turned away.

He caught her by the shoulders before she could put distance between them and brought her back against his body. "Is my presence in your bed so displeasing to you?" he murmured, his mouth at her ear.

She closed her eyes as pleasure shivered through her. "You know it is not. You are a very skilled lover. My body responds to you even when my mind wills differently. But the blood of the Karzana that runs in my veins demands I must be free to go to my people when they need me."

"*I* need you. Give me your love, Sharah."

"Gladly. When you give me my freedom."

He sighed heavily and gradually his hands loosened on her shoulders until they dropped to his side.

The heat between their bodies disturbed her. She took several steps away before she faced him again.

He pulled a red bag from the folds of his *candy.* "I have brought you a present that I have had made especially for you." She did not respond. Darius smiled inwardly. His Sharah—so stubborn, so proud. "Hold out your hands," he said softly, and when she did, he pulled the silken strings loose and upended the contents into her hand. Out spilled a long rope of large matched pearls. The clasp was a pearl that had grown in the shape of a heart.

Unable to stop the gasp of admiration that rose naturally to her lips, she lifted the necklace to the light. Each pearl was an object of perfect loveliness, creamy white in color, blushed with a soft pink.

Darius took them from her hands and carefully laid them around her neck. "These are my gift of love to you, Sharah," he said quietly.

She looked down at the pearls that fell over her breasts to reach to her knees, and within her proud soul another scar was carved. Darius had given her the extraordinary pearls to try to make her forget that even birds could fly free, but not she.

She raised her head, sending her hair rippling to her waist, a silken black cascade. "Am I free to do as I wish with these pearls?"

"Of course. They are yours."

She moved to one of the tall, arched tower windows. "Then I may throw them away?"

An expression of surprise crossed his face, but he nodded, wanting to humor her out of her sad mood. "Yes, although I wish you would not. It took a great deal of time and effort to collect pearls so perfectly matched."

"But may I throw them away?" she insisted.

Frowning, he said, "If you so desire."

She glanced out the window to the ground some hundreds of feet below. "And may I jump after them?"

"No!" Horrified, he raced across the room to pull her away from the window. "Sharah, what are you thinking of? If you jumped, you would be killed."

Gravely she stared up at him. "So I am free to do with the pearls what I will, but not myself."

"Sharah—"

"You gave me the pearls freely as a gift of your love. I, too, want to give you my love freely. But as long as I am kept against my will, I cannot.

"Sharah, how can I let you go?" His voice broke with his anguish. "You are my life."

She touched his face, so dear to her heart, and softly smiled. "No, Persia is your life. But you will have me, my dearest. Let me live as I was meant to be—free, like all those of my tribe, to shelter under the wide sky and ride with the winds. If you do this for me, I promise I will always come back to you."

"Sharah, I cannot . . ." He stopped as he saw her determined expression. "I have no choice, do I? I must surrender you to the sky and the winds if I am to keep you at all."

She gathered his strong hand in both of hers and raised it to brush the palm with her lips. "You won't be sorry. I may not always be here when you want me, but I will always be here for you when you need me."

And so Darius had his goldsmith put on the gold backing of the pearl clasp a special mark. It was two intertwining circles, without beginning or end, and symbolized Darius's and Sharah's eternal love for each other.

And for the rest of Darius's life Sharah came and went from the palace at will. It was reported that at his death, Sharah, wearing her lover's pearls, was by his bedside. Then she and the pearls disappeared, never to be seen again at the court of the Persians. But the story of their love and the pearls was told far and wide until it grew into legend.

One

St. Tropez
1989

The unexpected would happen tonight, Damon
Barand thought as he stood on the bridge of his
yacht and surveyed the scene around him. There
was something in the air—a volatility, an ener-
gized force—that raised the hairs on his skin and
told him to be on the alert. It was a feeling he had
been familiar with since the age of eight, and
when it came, he always paid attention. He was
alive today because he did.

His yacht, the commanding and formidable *Ares,*
rode at anchor on the after-midnight-dark water
in the harbor of St. Tropez. Lights were strung
like necklaces of sparkling diamonds from bow to
stern; more lights gleamed from every porthole.

Launches ferried guests back and forth from the quay to the ship over the black satin waters. An orchestra provided the music for the dancing on the main deck.

There was no sign of anything unusual as yet, but the feeling persisted in him.

"For once you might try enjoying one of these parties you're so famous for," he heard Graham Nader say behind him.

He didn't bother turning around him. "You don't feel it, do you, Graham?"

Graham stepped to the railing and gazed down on the party, considering the question. He'd been Damon's right-hand man for five years now; he knew more about him than most people did, which was not much at all. If he'd learned one thing, it was that the secrets of Damon's soul were obscured by dark, impenetrable mysteries. "Feel what?"

Damon cast him an enigmatic look, then switched his gaze to the party below, where elegantly dressed men and women swarmed over the deck. Their happy voices mixed with the music, while the varied hues of their evening finery swirled and swayed in kaleidoscopic designs and their jewels threw colored sparks out into the night.

Lifting his eyes to the shore, he saw the harbor lights of St. Tropez. Another port, another party. He wondered how many of both there had been. At this moment he couldn't recall why he had decided to have this party. "The animals are loose again."

Used to his employer's cynical view of the world, Graham's tone was amused. "Animals? Everyone on board tonight is either successful or wealthy or both. Royalty is mingling with major industrialists, movie stars, and models. I wouldn't call them animals."

"Perhaps we see them differently."

All at once Graham let out a long whistle. "Look at that girl down there!"

"Where?" Damon asked, only idly curious.

"There."

He followed the direction of Graham's finger to the dance area, where a young woman was currently burning up the floor with a sizzling version of the Charleston. People had backed away to form a circle around her and her partner, and were clapping and shouting encouragement to them.

"That's Prince Al Iraj dancing with her, isn't it?" Graham asked.

Damon didn't answer. With an unimpeded view of her, it took him mere seconds to expertly assess the young woman. She wasn't beautiful, but . . . she drew the eye because she possessed an infinitely watchable quality.

He bent and rested his forearms on the railing, studying her more closely. She was obviously having a good time, but her enjoyment of the party didn't seem to stem from the false gaiety around her or from the drinks that flowed like the Nile among his guests.

She laughed and tossed her head, treating him to the sight of a gleaming whirl of long auburn hair. A movement of her arms gave him a glimpse of high, firm breasts over the edge of the short, strapless, dark emerald-green velvet dress she wore. Then he caught a flash of long, shapely legs as she kicked, causing the dress's shimmering hot pink taffeta petticoat to flare about her knees.

And with her every movement a long rope of large, perfectly matched pearls swung back and forth across her breasts.

The rope of pearls was over seven feet long, Damon gauged, and it was too beautiful, too extravagant to make the average observer think it could be composed of real gems.

But he wasn't the average observer when it came to beautiful collectible things, and if he were right . . .

She had wrapped the pearls once around her neck so that the clasp, a large heart-shaped pearl, rested in the center of her throat. From this distance the color of the pearls appeared creamy white, but he believed that a closer inspection would reveal a blush of soft pink in them.

If he were right, the pearls she wore were the fabulous, elusive, priceless Pearls of Sharah. And if that were so, the unexpected had indeed happened tonight.

He had once seen a rare photograph of the pearls. Shortly after that photograph had been taken in the 1930s, the pearls had disappeared again. The Pearls of Sharah were the ultimate prize for any collector.

"Isn't she something?" Graham said. "She's not

the raving-beauty type that usually attracts you, but she's got a kind of sparkle and vivacity that puts most of the women here to shame."

If he were right, Damon thought, he would do everything in his power to insure that the Pearls of Sharah would soon be his.

Perplexed by his employer's continued silence, Graham asked, "What is it?"

"The pearls," Damon said, straightened, and started off.

"Wait," Graham called. "Delgado is due any minute."

Damon lifted a hand. "Let me know when he arrives."

Breathless with laughter, Alexandra Sheldon collapsed against her darkly handsome escort, Prince Zander Al Iraj. "You've been practicing."

Zan gathered together the considerable dignity he had at his command. "You are the only one with whom I dance the Charleston. It is a sacred thing we share, I swear it."

"Then I obviously taught you too well." She pushed off her forehead the auburn hair that had fallen into her eyes as she gazed around her. "You know, I have the strangest sensation. The air is almost electric tonight. Do you feel it too?"

Heir to an oil-rich kingdom and already world-weary at the age of twenty-six due to an excess of everything money could buy, Zan glanced indifferently at the people around him on the dance floor. As he did, he automatically registered the efforts of several beautiful women who were working to gain his attention. "Nothing unusual."

"The very air seems alive with possibilities." She laughed, more at herself than at anything else. "I don't know. Maybe it's just being aboard this yacht. I've never seen anything like this. It's magnificent."

Only when Zan looked at Alex did his indifference disappear. "The *Ares* is the largest privately owned yacht in the world. My father has the second largest." He grinned. "It often bothers him to be second, but Damon Barand doesn't appear to care. He isn't a man to engage in competition or one-upmanship. The things he does he does only for himself."

"He sounds interesting. How well do you know him?"

"I know him only by reputation. My father does business with Barand, and when the great man heard that I was in St. Tropez on holiday, he invited me to this party."

"Great man?"

"It is said that Damon Barand has more power than many governments."

Alex regarded her sumptuous surroundings with lively interest. "And more money, no doubt."

In a playful gesture he ran a finger lightly down Alex's freckled nose. "He's a billionaire, my pet, but if all it took to impress you was money, I would have had you in my bed the first day we met at school."

She squeezed his arm affectionately. "Getting women into your bed is and always has been infinitely easy for you, Zan. Lovers come and go, but friends are forever. At the time we met, you needed a friend more than you did a lover, and so did I. We still need each other as friends. Admit it."

Not used to confessing anything to a woman, Zan raised an imperious brow. It was a reflexive act, but the sight of Alex eyeing him with amusement pulled him up short, and he threw back his head and laughed. "I admit it. And I also admit that I've missed you terribly. You're fresh air to me, and you're one of the few people with whom I can totally relax and forget my position."

With an ease of long familiarity Alex rose up on tiptoe and kissed Zan's cheek. "And I've missed you. Since we've been out of school, I don't get to see you nearly enough."

He grimaced. "We have too many responsibilities. This holiday together was a great idea. Both of us needed a break, but especially you. Since Charlotte's death, you've been living at the office."

"Yes, but it's what I've needed. Her death left a hole in my life, and continuing the work that meant so much to her helped fill that gap."

Just then a woman raced by them, shrieking in delight as a man chased after her. The woman was wearing nothing but a tablecloth and the man chasing her wore a life preserver.

Zan's Persian blue eyes twinkled with mischief. "Shall we join in the fun?"

"I'm extremely fond of what I'm wearing," Alex

warned. "And I've never looked my best in a tablecloth."

With a chuckle he hooked his hands under her arms and swung her around and up until she was standing on one of the refreshment tables.

"Zan, you're incorrigible!"

"That's what my father says."

"Really?"

"Well . . . not in those exact words."

"I bet."

"Excuse me."

The sound of a deep voice behind her made Alex pivot too fast. Trying to keep her balance among an array of crystal champagne glasses and hors d'oeuvre-ladened silver trays proved to be a lost cause. She teetered and fell backwards, right into a pair of strong, masculine arms.

"Ohhh!"

"Hello."

Eyes as mysterious and black as the sea around them stared down at her, mesmerizing her with their intensity in an instant. "Hello," she whispered.

"Having a good time?" He shifted her weight so that her breasts were pressed into his chest, and a strange kind of burning started in her heart.

"I'm having a wonderful time," she said, bewildered by her reaction. She studied the stranger for clues. His face was intriguing—the skin deeply tanned, the cheekbones, nose, and chin sharp and angular . . . a face formed by harsh, furious forces. It was not a handsome face or a face that inspired ease, but she was entranced by it. She felt as though something monumental were happening to her. "Thank you, by the way. You just saved me from disgrace."

One eyebrow rose. "Surely not."

She grinned. "I'm afraid it's true. I was about to fall face first into the pâté de foie gras, and I'm sure the owner of this fabulous yacht would have had me tossed overboard."

His lips curved into a smile so intimate, she had a sudden urge to believe he had never smiled like that at any other woman. Fully aware that she was being foolish, she silently chided herself. But then he spoke again.

"On the contrary. The owner of this yacht would have enjoyed rescuing you and licking the pâté de foie gras off you, bit by bit."

Like gasoline poured over embers, his words ignited shooting flames within her that stole the oxygen from her body. "You're Damon Barand, aren't you?"

He nodded. "And you are?"

"Alexandra Sheldon . . . Alex."

"Alexandra."

He said her name as if tasting it. The need to put air into her lungs made her inhale deeply, but the act unintentionally pushed her breasts harder against him, causing her nipples to stiffen and begin to ache. "You can release me now."

Damon's gaze dropped to her throat and followed the line of the pearls until they disappeared between their two bodies. Each pearl in and of itself was a showpiece, but strung together and perfectly matched to the rest, they were incredible.

His pulse quickened at the discovery. "I could release you," he agreed. "But, you see, I don't want to."

She felt as if she had waited all her life for just this moment . . . for just this man. She wanted to stay in his arms . . . and stay and stay and stay.

Her mouth went quite naturally into a soft, sweet smile. "I'm comfortable if you are."

Something stirred in Damon, and he knew a momentary disquiet. What was it? Intriguing flecks of gold glimmered warmly in the softness of her brown eyes, catching his attention.

Then there was the unusual luminous glow of her skin. No, he thought, immediately correcting himself. Her skin couldn't be that radiant. The unique glow he was seeing had to be a reflection from the glorious pearls.

But there *was* something else. Her auburn hair had fallen away from her face, exposing a bad-looking scar that ran a little over two inches along her left jaw and disappeared behind her ear. He dropped the arm he had hooked around her waist, and she slowly slid down and away from his body.

Relieved yet disappointed to have space between them, Alex glanced toward Zan and discovered him grinning at her. She turned back to Damon Barand. "Have you met Prince Al Iraj?"

"I haven't had the pleasure." Damon extended his hand. "Prince Al Iraj. I know your father well, of course."

"Call me Zan, and thank you for the invitation tonight."

"Thank you for bringing Alex," he said smoothly, returning his attention to her.

He believed she was Zan's date, and he didn't care, she realized. His disregard of a man who might have a prior claim on her was a surprise. And a thrill. Zan had said, the things Damon Barand does he does only for himself.

A movement of Damon's hand brought a waiter to their side. "Champagne?"

She already felt drunk. "This air is intoxicating enough for me."

"The air?"

"Can't you feel it? There's an effervescence in the air."

"Is that what it is?" he asked.

"Excuse me, Damon."

The dark intensity of Damon's gaze never left her, but he spoke to the blond-haired man who had come up behind him. "What is it, Graham?"

"Your appointment."

Damon lifted his hand to her throat and slowly brushed her flesh. She inhaled sharply and felt a wave of heat tremble through her. Then he skimmed his fingers down the suddenly sensitive skin until he encountered the pearl clasp. Lightly he rubbed it.

"Wait for me?"

She nodded, still feeling the imprint of his fingers on her skin. He had touched her so gently, yet she was sure he must have left marks.

He smiled at her. "Good."

Caught up in his mystical spell, she watched

him weave his way through his guests and disappear through a door. She had never seen a man who could move so elegantly, she decided, yet who had such a predatory way of looking at a person. The combination was devastating.

"You're playing with fire," Zan said.

"Am I?"

"Alexandra, you've never in all your life come up against anything or anyone like Damon Barand. He's everything in the world you want to avoid. Let's leave." When she didn't move, he took her by the shoulders and stared into her eyes. "You're not listening to me. Let's go back to the hotel."

It seemed as if the effervescent air had filled suddenly with shadows, blocking everything but Damon's image from her vision. "Why do you want to leave?" she asked.

Zan gave an exasperated sigh. "Barand is an arms merchant, Alex. His business is death. His only home is this yacht, which constantly sails from port to port so that no one is ever sure where he'll be next. His personal life is just as unpredictable and unstable, involving a steady stream of women. He can't be pinned down in any way that counts. Do you understand? He's a very dangerous man."

Her gaze cleared, and she saw the earnest expression on Zan's handsome face. "I believe you. But he asked me to wait for him. Where's the harm?"

"Lord, you're stubborn." Zan pulled a gold cigarette case from his jacket pocket, extracted a brown cigarette, and lit it. "Remember the time you borrowed my new sports car and I warned you about the speed? You didn't listen and ended up in the hospital for ten days."

"I recovered, and I offered to buy you a new car."

"I didn't care about the car. I did and do care about you. You recovered from the accident, but you might not be so fortunate this time."

"I repeat, he only asked me to wait for him."

"Do you really think that's all he asked?"

She looked away from him. "No." After a moment she added, "You underestimate me, Zan."

He exhaled a heavy stream of smoke. "No, I don't. You're one of the strongest women I know, but I happen to know the trauma you went through to get such strength. You don't need the grief this man could bring you." Suddenly he gave a disgusted snort. "For heaven's sake, Alex. For years I've watched all sorts of men try to get to you. Why now? Why *him*?"

Lovingly she raised a hand to his cheek. "You ask me that? You, who's always expounded that Middle Eastern fatalism of yours? How many times have you told me man cannot alter that which is predetermined?"

He smiled wryly. "Many times, but you never listened. You've always said you didn't believe in fate."

"Well . . . perhaps I do now. After all"—she waved her hand in the direction that Damon had disappeared—"what other explanation can there be?"

He shook his head. "Alex, you don't know what you're doing."

"I know," she said slowly.

In the very heart of the ship, in a leather and teak study behind a large desk, Damon lazed, perfectly at ease in the comfort of a custom-made Cordovan leather chair. But his black eyes were as hard as the onyx inlay of the desktop. To the four men who watched him so intently, Damon Barand looked as lazy as a cobra about to strike a victim.

Feeling a great and imminent peril in his bones, Emilio Delgado knew himself to be the victim. But still, as Barand idly twirled an emerald-and-ruby-encrusted dagger that Emilio had seen Barand use as a letter opener, Emilio couldn't help but hope that he was wrong. The arms buy he had set up for the Rayos was of vital importance to him because of the great sum of money he would clear on the deal, and to the revolutionary group if they were to continue their fight.

Suddenly and without warning, the dagger whizzed by Emilio's left ear, so close that his skin felt the chill of the steel blade. Ten feet behind him, the blade embedded itself into the teak-paneled wall with a deadly thud, and he knew that his instincts about the peril had been right. Despite all his efforts, Barand somehow had found out for whom the arms were intended.

Slowly Damon leaned forward until his forearms were resting on the edge of his desk. The gentleness with which he spoke didn't even begin to belie the gleaming ice that was in his eyes. "It wasn't even a good try, Emilio."

"Really, I don't know what you're talking—"

Damon's hand came down on the desk with enough force to stop Emilio's next words. "I said I wouldn't deal with the Rayos. Evidently you weren't listening, or you thought I was a fool and you could get around me. Either way, you've been extremely unwise."

With a weak smile Emilio tried to shrug off his mistake. "I'm sorry. It's just that—"

"I told you from the start that I'm selective about who ends up with the arms I sell."

"Be reasonable, Barand. What the hell difference can it make? The guns will kill no matter who they're sold to."

The minute the words were out, Emilio realized he should have kept his mouth shut. The look on Barand's face almost froze the blood pumping through Emilio's veins.

"Try some other line of work, Emilio, because you're as good as dead in this one. From this moment on, neither my friends nor my enemies will do business with you."

Emilio jumped up, anger shaking his entire body. "They may be afraid of you, Barand, but I'm not. And I'm warning you now, your control over the arms that are bought and sold in this part of the world is almost at an end. Soon I will be sitting where you are."

Damon pressed a button on his desk, and in the next second two men entered the study with guns drawn. "Good-bye, Emilio," Damon said softly.

Emilio threw the man behind the desk a glance filled with hate and stalked out of the room, followed closely by the two men who had been sitting silently on either side of him.

Graham, who had been leaning against the wall behind Damon, pushed away and moved until he was standing in front of the desk. "You haven't heard the last of him. He's an extremely unpleasant person."

Damon's sigh was so faint it was almost inaudible. "When have I ever dealt with any other kind?" He stood and slid his hands into the pockets of his dinner jacket.

"Emilio Delgado is different. He was aware of your policy to deal with only those countries or regimes of which you approve. The very fact that he still tried to deceive you proves that he's a man to beware of."

"Delgado is a fool who lets greed overrule prudence." The grim line of his mouth softened slightly. "Forget him, and let's go back to the party. I have someone waiting for me."

Alex stood at the side of the dance floor, watching Zan and a dark-haired beauty move to the music. He was a good dancer, she thought with pride. But then, she'd been the one who had taught him to dance, starting with lessons at their first freshman mixer. They'd been two lonely kids, each feeling displaced.

A man approached her. "Dance?"

"No, thank you," she said as she had to several men since Damon had left.

Fingering a pearl at her neck, she gazed up at the night sky, where a million stars burned and where, if the theory of fatalism was correct, destinies were decided. Was that what had happened? Had the fates decreed before she was born that one electrifying night on the Côte d'Azur, she would look into a pair of black eyes and find a powerful force she could not resist?

Maybe. Maybe not.

Perhaps she shouldn't try so hard to find an explanation. After all, Charlotte had spent years unlocking the portions of Alex's mind and soul that the accident had closed, teaching her to be open and aware to the beautiful potential of life.

"Will you dance with me?"

With thudding heart Alex turned and smiled up at Damon. Her wait was at an end. "I'd love to," she said softly.

As he led her to the dance area, the throbbing beat of a rock song blared. They found a position among the wildly gyrating couples, and he drew her against his body and held her without moving. "The music is about to change," he explained.

He raised his hand and snapped his fingers. Astonishingly the band segued smoothly into a ballad with a richly layered sound that twined around them and seemed to change the energy of the night. Suddenly images and impressions were lifted above the ordinary and the senses dominated. Or maybe being in Damon's arms had done that, she thought. His strength and heat were taking possession of her, penetrating her skin, making her feel warm and lethargic as if she'd just slipped into a vat of heated honey. His hand slid down her back and pressed against her hips, melding her to his hard pelvis.

"I hate dancing," he murmured, staring down into her eyes, "but I wanted an excuse to feel your body against mine."

Many men had tried to seduce her, and Alex had always responded with poise and good-natured humor. But now she found herself speechless.

"What I'd really like to do," he continued, "is to strip off every fragment of your clothing and *then* feel you against me."

He was saying the most outrageous things, Alex realized, as if they were the most ordinary. She glanced around the luxurious yacht, then back to him. "I suppose you always get what you want."

"Always," he whispered.

She nodded, thinking that what she was about to say made no sense but knowing that she was going to say it anyway. "Well, then, I suppose you will get me."

She had no idea what would have happened next between them, because it was then, out of the corner of her eye, that she saw the gun. Held in the hand of a wild-eyed man who was dressed as a waiter, it was pointed straight at the back of Damon's head.

Holding Alex as closely as he was, Damon felt her tense, and he saw her face whiten and her lips move soundlessly. Simultaneously he heard a voice from behind him yell, "*Long live the Rayos!*"

In the time it takes a bolt of lightning to streak from heaven to earth, he shoved Alex to the floor, then twisted around, his arms stiff, palm flat, and knocked the gun out of the surprised man's hand. Hooking his foot behind the man's left leg, he yanked and the man went down. In a matter of seconds it was all over.

Well-dressed guards converged on the man, jerked him up, and dragged him away. The orchestra never stopped playing. Lying on the floor, stunned, it seemed to Alex that people had barely paused. If it weren't for the gun at her feet, she might have thought she had imagined it.

Then she felt Zan lift her to her feet. "Are you all right?"

She nodded mutely, her eyes seeking and finding Damon. The man he had called Graham was with him, listening closely to what Damon was saying. Finally Graham whirled and moved purposefully away.

Zan's arms closed protectively around her. "Come on, I'll take you back to your hotel."

"I—"

Damon returned immediately to her side. "I'm sorry about all this, Alex. I hated to have to push you like that, but it was necessary. Are you hurt?"

"I don't think so."

"That fall had to have jarred. I'd feel better if a doctor looked at you."

"No, really, I'm just shaken. It will pass." She waited a moment until she had successfully forced some of the tension from her body. "Who was that man anyway?"

"A member of a fanatical revolutionary group with whom I refuse to do business. Don't be concerned. He won't bother us again."

"I think I should take her back to the hotel," Zan said.

Damon held her gaze. "Is that what you want, Alex?"

"I . . . no . . . I'd like to stay."

"Good." A slow smile evoked a subtle transformation in Damon, changing his hard mouth into lines that were staggeringly sensual. "Perhaps you'd like to see some of the *Ares*."

"I'd like that very much. Zan?"

Zan stepped between her and Damon and took her face between his hands. "All right," he whispered, "but, Alexandra, take care, and I'll see you later."

Two

Damon thoughtfully watched Zan's departure, then he looked back at Alexandra. "I would have expected more of an argument from the prince."

She tilted her head so that a gleaming spill of auburn hair slid over one bare shoulder. "Would it have mattered if he had argued?"

"Not to me." He paused. "Do you think his attitude will still be as cavalier when he realizes I'm not going to bring you back to him?"

She regarded him steadily. "If he knows I want to stay with you, then he'll be happy for me."

"It sounds like the two of you have an unusual relationship."

"Zan and I met during our first year at college. He helped me with the insecurity and loneliness I felt at being away from home for the first time, and I helped him with the culture shock he experienced. We've been close friends ever since."

"Friends." Without warning he lifted a finger to stroke down the pearls. With his eyes fixed on their splendor, he said, "You saved my life, Alexandra."

He had one hand tucked casually in the pocket of his black evening trousers, the other on the pearls that lay over her breast. Her head spun with his nearness. Every word he spoke, every gesture he made, seemed suggestive of lovemaking. "I didn't do a thing. It was you. I've never seen anyone move so fast in my life."

"Nevertheless, it was your expression that alerted me to the danger. Therefore, it was you who saved my life."

The thought of him lying at her feet, his life's blood draining out of him, made her ill. "Then I'm glad I did. The incident could have had a tragic end." She shook her head. "I've never been exposed to true violence. I don't think many people have been."

His face became granitelike. "Ah, but you are wrong. Everyone is surrounded by violence. Some are just more aware of it than others."

Juxtapositioned with his harshly spoken words was the gentleness of his fingers which strayed from the pearls onto the velvet of the dress, then upward to the bare skin above the low neckline. Alex closed her eyes as the heated sensation of his touch filtered into her body. She wished the people and noise that surrounded them gone so that she and Damon could be alone.

She opened her eyes just as he was lowering his head toward her. He brushed his lips across her cheek to her ear. "Let me show you my home," he whispered.

Desire shivered through her and she was aware that if he'd said, *let me take off your clothes and make love to you in the middle of the dance floor*, she would have agreed.

She'd never had a lover.

She'd never been in love.

But the black satin night overflowed with rich promises, and she was in the dark, swirling center of it, unwilling, unable to fight her way out.

He held her hand as he led her through the grand salon, a hall, then up a stairway and into a large, opulently furnished salon above the main deck. "This is where my private quarters start."

Like streams flowing together to unite, so, too, did the diverse elements of the room. Six old-master paintings hung on the wall behind the large U-shaped sofa that was covered by deep purple Scalamandré brocade. A tall Louis XIV chest inlaid with tortoiseshell and ivory stood against a far wall, and in another part of the remarkable room, a long malachite table waited for dinner to be served on it. And everywhere there were fine works of art.

"You have so many treasures," she said, breathless at the beauty around her. She broke away from Damon and went immediately to a Fabergé egg. The egg lay open to reveal an intricately wrought golden sailing ship.

"That was presented to Maria Fedorovna by Alexander III in 1891," Damon said. "The egg itself is made from a solid piece of heliotrope jasper."

"It's amazing," she said softly, studying the detail.

"Tell me about yourself," she heard him say as she moved to stand before a jade and gold lion with rose diamond eyes.

"What would you like to know?"

"What do you do when you're not on holiday with the prince?"

"I own and run a cosmetics company in Connecticut. It was my grandmother, Charlotte's, company, and I inherited it when she passed away last year."

"And you run this company by yourself?"

She shot him an amused look. "You sound amazed."

"You're very young."

She passed before a case filled with gem-encrusted silver chalices. "Twenty-six, and I do have an excellent manager upon whom I depend. But I've worked in the company for years, starting when I was nine, after school and in the summers. I know every aspect of the business thoroughly."

"So you sell beauty."

"And you obviously collect beauty." She had stopped to admire a gold rose bush on a gold-footed stand. The roses were inset with sapphires and rubies and the whole bush was about thirty inches high. "What a delicate piece. The artist must have been very attuned to nature. Look at the perfect way each petal is shaped and veined."

"It's fifteenth century," he said.

She next paused before a statue of a nude woman who had been caught in the act of laying her drapery on an urn beside her. "It's Aphrodite, isn't it?"

"Yes. The Greek goddess of sensuality."

"And love." Alex let her hand flow over the statue's contours. "The sculpture is just incredible, isn't it? The lines of the body are so smooth, yet you can actually feel the individual strands of her hair." Her tone was reverent. "When you touch this statue, you're touching the person who carved it all those centuries ago."

Watching her, listening to her, Damon realized with a jolt that he had never so much as put a hand on the statue. Yet Alex was receiving more pleasure from her brief moments of contact with it than he had received in all the years he had owned it. And she had seen veins on the gold rose petals when he never had. The knowledge bothered him in some vague way.

She switched her attention to a painting of a moonlit scene. "You can almost feel the glow of the moon, can't you? The artist's brush strokes create an atmosphere that invites you in—"

"Alex."

His voice had the hushed and gentle murmur of a slow-moving brook, she thought, and turned to discover a strange look of hunger on his face as he gazed at the painting. But it didn't make sense. He *owned* the painting. The moment passed.

"Let's go out on the afterdeck," he said.

"All right."

Again he held out his hand—a simple, unthreatening gesture from a complex, dangerous man—and she couldn't help but put her hand in his and follow him into the next room. His bedroom.

Intimate and sensuous was her first thought. Unexpected was her next. The oversize bed sat on a dove-gray plushly carpeted pedestal and was spread with an oyster-colored-satin comforter. The chairs and couch had no harsh or discordant lines. Crisp taffeta, soft suede, raw silk, and reflective mirrors covered the walls with a range of subtle twilight hues of gray and mauve.

She would never have predicted such a room from a man with his occupation, she thought. Suddenly she had the eerie feeling that she had just dived into a beautiful sea where a shark circled and waited. Beauty and death.

For the last few hours she had reacted instinctively, suspending reason and logic, but now that same instinct was telling her she needed to know more. "Your ship is appropriately named, Damon. Ares was the Greek god of war, wasn't he?"

"Yes."

"Tell me something. Why do you do it? Why do you sell weapons?"

He almost smiled. Strangely no one had ever asked him that question. "The world's a powder keg, Alex. At least by doing what I do I can control which part of the world has the fuses."

"That's a rationalization."

"Yes. And it's also the truth."

To take on the responsibility of trying to control the violence in the world, whether he was right or not, was something an ordinary man would never do. Alex wished with all her heart that Damon wasn't so extraordinary. She glanced once more around the room. "There are no windows."

He raised his hand to outline the shape of her lips. "A precaution. A man is at his most vulnerable when he's sleeping . . . or making love."

Her breath caught. "I can't imagine you ever being vulnerable."

"Can you imagine me making love . . . to you?"

Her throat constricted. If she had been able to speak, her reply would have been an unequivocal yes. And she had the feeling that he knew this, but he remained silent.

He led her through another door and out onto a deck that was at the other end of the ship from where the party was being held. Deep plump chairs and couches were arranged around the deck, and a canopy covered half the area.

Damon lit two tall, fat candles and placed crystal globes over them to protect the golden flames from the night wind. Then he shrugged out of his jacket, tossed it aside, and drew her down onto the many-pillowed couch that had the bulkhead at its back. Resting his arm on the pillowed back, he shifted slightly so that he was facing her.

Faint strains of the music being played on the main deck reached them, but they seemed completely isolated, surrounded by sea and darkness, just as Damon had planned. He had wanted to separate her from Zan, to get her all to himself.

Against her fair skin and emerald-velvet dress, the pearls gleamed with an incredible richness and depth. Infinitely desirable. The pearls. Alex.

Alex knew what it was like to be afraid and nervous, and what she was feeling now included a bit of both of those emotions, plus hope, and a very real need, and it all came to the sum total of anticipation. She smoothed the emerald velvet of her skirt in a betraying gesture. "When will the party end?"

His hand closed over hers and brought the soft underside of her wrist to his mouth. He felt her pulse jump. "Actually," he said, "I gave the signal to end the party before we left the dance floor. Launches have already begun carrying the guests back to shore."

"Why did you do that?"

"I was no longer interested in the party."

"Were you ever?"

He smiled at her perceptiveness. "No. Not until I saw you."

"You take my breath away," she whispered.

His smile disappeared, and he tensed. Her complete naturalness was one of the most erotic stimulants he had ever known. "You don't put up any guard, do you?"

"I must sound very naive, but I don't think I

could play games with you even if I wanted to. The truth is, something happened when I looked into your eyes that I'm still trying to figure out. I'm sure I should raise some sort of guard against you, but, you see, I can't."

He lifted their still-joined hands so that he could brush the pad of one finger down her cheek. "You're very frank, very open."

"And you're used to more sophisticated banter."

"I like the way you talk." As he lowered their hands, he trailed the one finger over her jaw, down her neck, to the top of the dress. She took a deep breath, pulling air into her lungs. Her breasts rose above the neckline of her dress, and his finger dipped to flick against a rigid nipple. Gasping, she briefly closed her eyes, and he felt a searing pleasure surge through his veins.

Abruptly he dropped her hand. He had acted before he could think and now he silently cursed himself.

The magnificent necklace skimmed her breasts to end in a shimmering pool in her lap. He scooped the luminiscent mass of pearls into his hand. "This is an extraordinary necklace. Would you mind if I studied it more closely."

Surprise made her answer come a beat late. "No, I don't mind at all." She unwound the necklace from around her neck, unhooked the clasp, and handed it to him.

He held the pearls toward the candles. The glow illuminated the rich luster of each pearl and the gold backing of the clasp, clearly showing the jeweler's mark of the two circles, intertwined for all eternity.

He had been right. He held in his hands the Pearls of Sharah.

His heart was pounding so that he could barely hear what Alexandra was saying.

"You know, it's very strange, but Zan seems to feel something when he looks at my necklace." She chuckled. "I tell him it's that royal Persian blood of his. Any blood so old and so blue is bound to make a person crazy sooner or later."

"Has the prince seen this marking on the back of the clasp?" he asked carefully.

"Yes, and he's offered to have one of the scholars in his country research it for me. Maybe I'll do that someday, but for now I'm happy just to have them and wear them. You see, they were my grandmother's. Like the cosmetics company, I inherited the pearls from Charlotte."

"And where did she get them?"

She gave a light laugh. "I'm not sure. I was going through her things one day and came across a velvet pouch shoved way back in the corner of one of her drawers. The pearls were in the pouch. I'd forgotten all about them."

"You'd seen them before?"

"Years ago, when I was a small child, she showed them to me. She told me that they were very special and that their beauty wasn't in their appearance or value but rather in the feeling behind them. Then she put them away. I didn't fully understand what she meant until much later."

He looked at her strangely, and she hesitated, but when he didn't say anything, she decided to continue with her story. "I've spent a lot of time speculating about how these pearls came to be in Charlotte's possession. She never mentioned them again, and no one I know ever saw her wear them. My grandfather died right after I was born, and by all accounts the two of them were very happy together. But I'm certain the pearls weren't a gift from him."

"How can you be so sure?"

She shrugged. "I think she would have worn them more if they had been from him. No, it's my theory that she had a secret lover who gave them to her. For some reason, she and this man couldn't come out into the open with their love and so she wore them only when she was with him."

"A very romantic theory."

She grinned. "I know, but to me it makes perfect sense, and I'm honored Charlotte left them to me. They make me feel warm and close to her."

"Let me buy the necklace from you."

She eyed him uncertainly, noticing that he was stroking one of the pearls with the same finger he'd used to stroke her. "You're joking."

"No, I'm not. I want to buy them."

Somewhat uncomfortable at the turn of the conversation, she shook her head firmly. "They're not for sale. They were my grandmother's."

"But you just said she never wore them, and evidently she cared so little for them, she kept them in the back of a drawer."

"You're wrong about her not caring. It was obvious to me even as a young girl that she treasured them. And even if she hadn't, it doesn't matter. They were hers, and I would never sell them."

"I'll pay a great deal of money for them."

She was suddenly aware that the music had stopped. "No."

Damon placed the pearls in her lap and drew away from her, for the moment stymied but not defeated. In fact, he was elated: Alex had no idea what she had in those pearls.

Alex blinked, unsure of what had just happened. If Damon hadn't settled back into the corner of the couch, the light from the candles would never have touched his face in such a way that made it possible for her to see the grim determination in his expression. As it was, the glimpse was brief, and in the next instant Alex decided she'd been imagining it.

"Your grandmother sounds like a remarkable woman," he said.

Alex flipped her hair up and put on the necklace. "She was. She raised me with love that was without conditions, and she taught me many important lessons about life. I miss her very much."

"I'm sure you do. But you saw her as your grandmother. The man who gave her those pearls would have seen her through the eyes of a lover. She must have been a very passionate woman." He paused. "Like her granddaughter."

A small thrill stung her. "You don't know that."

"Yes, I do."

It was so quiet, too quiet. Alex could hear only the lapping of the water against the hull and the pounding of her heart. She moistened her lips and turned her head away.

He brushed her hair back over her ear and briefly caressed her earlobe. "Everyone's gone. Even Zan. Does that bother you?"

She looked back at him. "No."

His lips quirked. "So you're not only passionate, you're brave as well."

"Perhaps I'm neither."

"You're both and more, I'm sure."

His attention was totally focused on her, bathing her in a high concentration of energy and heat that threatened to burn her. She decided to try to deflect at least a portion of it. "Turnabout is fair play, Damon. I can also make a few assumptions about you. For instance, a man such as yourself who has a constantly moving yacht as his home is obviously a man who needs no people, no roots."

"Really?"

"Really. And the business in which you engage is so ugly you have a need to surround yourself with beautiful things."

She wasn't telling him anything he didn't know, but her answer to his next two questions would tell him something about her. "You think the selling of arms is an ugly business?" he asked softly.

"Yes."

"If that's so, Alexandra Sheldon, what are you doing here?"

Her answer came with surprising quickness.

"I'm here because of you, not the business you're in."

Blood drummed in his temples. Every woman he could think of would have delivered that line as a come-on, but she was being totally honest with him. Where was her artifice, he questioned with something like wonder.

Could it be remotely possible that *she* was the something unexpected for which his feeling had told him to be on the alert? His gaze fastened on the pearls. No, she couldn't be.

"Dawn is breaking," he said.

He was like the dark side of the moon, she thought. She could see his face, but she had no idea what was behind it. And like the moon, he exerted a powerful force, drawing her closer and closer to him.

Feeling restless, needing to break away from his relentless pull, she rose and walked to the railing. The sky was already beginning to lighten, casting a shading of gold over the harbor. Small yachts and fishing boats filled the little square of water, and the gentle sway of their masts was barely perceptible. Cafés and restaurants lined the waterfront, their facades closed, their awnings rolled back. Behind the Quai Jean Jaurès were tall, narrow houses, washed in cream, pink, and ochre.

She heard Damon behind her.

"We'll be lifting anchor soon."

When she turned, she found him a few feet away. The early morning light bathed the bronze-skinned angles of his face, turning them gold but not lessening their severity.

"Do you want to go ashore?"

There it was—the question for which, however subtly it was phrased, she had been unconsciously waiting for hours.

Up until that moment she hadn't known how she would respond.

She linked her fingers together and regarded her hands briefly. "Once again, I don't know how to be anything but honest with you, Damon. Tonight has been disturbing on many levels. A lot has happened. I feel that somehow you've woven a bejeweled sensual web around me. There seems to be an inevitability about this night that's almost overpowering."

Damon nodded in a show of understanding, but he was privately irritated by how tensely he awaited her decision. His throat had gone dry, and his hands had clenched until he had had to shove them into his pockets.

She gave a light, embarrassed laugh. "What I'm trying to say—and I'm doing it very badly—is that I'd very much like to stay, but . . . I need time to catch my breath. I—I'd like my own stateroom."

His hesitation was barely noticeable. "Of course."

She let out a soundless sigh of relief. She hadn't wanted to leave, but, ensnared by him though she was, she had to be sure of what she was doing. Because, she knew, if she decided to sleep with him, she would change her life forever.

He lifted the receiver of a phone fastened to the bulkhead. "What hotel are you staying at?"

"Le Mas de Chastelas. Zan and I have one of the bungalows."

"See that Miss Sheldon's luggage is collected immediately from Le Mas de Chastelas and brought here," he said into the phone, then hung up.

As sure as she was about her decision, she was also nervous. "I should call Zan myself."

"Perhaps you're right. Do you know the number?"

"No."

He lifted the receiver again. "Connect Miss Sheldon with Le Mas de Chastelas, Prince Al Iraj's bungalow," he said, and handed her the phone. Then he walked to the railing to give her privacy.

"Hello." Zan's voice was gruff.

Either he had been asleep or she had interrupted something, she thought. Perhaps the dark-haired beauty he had been dancing with . . . "Hi, it's me. I just wanted to tell you that there'll be someone by for my luggage soon. I've decided to stay on board the *Ares*."

"Well, hell, Alex." It was a drawl that had a multitude of shadings.

She couldn't help but smile. "Sometimes you sound so Western."

"And sometimes you sound so—I don't suppose it'd do me any good to tell you that you're out of your mind."

"None whatsoever."

"All right, then I'll save my breath. But remember that I'm just a phone call away. No matter where I am, you can always reach me through the palace."

"I know. And thanks. I'll talk to you soon."

"Promise?"

"I promise." She replaced the receiver. Damon had undone his tie and several buttons on his shirt. The casualness of his appearance hit her already aroused senses as devastatingly sexy.

"Everything all right?" he asked, walking to her.

"Fine."

When he was in front of her, he took her face in his hands. "Alex," he said gently, "your face is too expressive for me to believe you. What's wrong? Is it Zan?"

"No." She moistened her bottom lip with her tongue and decided it was only right that she tell him. "When . . . if . . . we make love, it will be my first time."

A feeling that was simultaneously sharp and shimmering wove through his system and tangled in his gut. "Maybe it *was* you, after all," he said.

"What?"

"I had a feeling something unexpected would happen tonight."

She wrapped her hand around his wrist. "It did. You were nearly killed, or have you forgotten?"

"I haven't forgotten, but that was expected." Slowly he lowered his head and covered her mouth with his.

It was their first kiss and an experience for which Alex had been hungering all night. Like the new day dawning around her, passion awakened within her. Brimming over with the wonder of it, she clung to him, stubbornly pushing away all thought of possible heartbreak. If it came, she would deal with it. Until then . . .

"There's nothing for you to be afraid of," he said against her mouth, his breath caressing her lips. "When we make love, you'll have no cause for concern. I will protect you and make sure there will be no accidents from our lovemaking."

Three

The *Ares* was under way when Alex awoke. She sat up and gazed around the stateroom Damon had led her to early this morning. The cabin was decorated in the pastel colors of sunrise.

Damon's stateroom was cloaked by twilight colors and had no windows.

On the bedside table was a button marked "drapes." She pushed it, and the heavy rose-hued silk drapes drew back to reveal a bank of windows along the outside wall. The night before she had seen St. Tropez from those windows. Today there was only open sea.

For a brief moment a sense of isolation threatened her, but she firmly pushed away the feeling. She was far from isolated. Last night Damon had told her that she could call anywhere in the world from any room on the ship due to a satellite telex and telephone link. Besides, staying aboard the *Ares* had been her decision. Damon had given her what she wanted—her own stateroom, and time to catch her breath and get to know him. Everything was going to be fine.

A panel on the bedside table lifted and a solid gold phone rose to within easy reach. Alex stared at it, fascinated. When it rang, she jumped.

"Hello?" she answered tentatively.

"Miss Sheldon, I am Benes, and I hope I have not disturbed you," came the polite, heavily accented male voice. "Mr. Barand said I should wait until this time to inquire after you."

"I see." She gazed toward the windows. "Could you please tell me what time is it?"

"It is four o'clock, Miss Sheldon, and if it is convenient for you, Mr. Barand would like you to join him in one hour in the grand salon."

Her heart rate picked up. "Tell him I'd be happy to."

Damon flipped the dagger into the air, let it revolve once, then caught it again by its gem-encrusted handle. Graham had watched Damon repeat that action for a good ten minutes, but Graham knew Damon's mind was not on the dagger. Damon's next question proved it.

"Who do you think is responsible for the hijacking?"

"No one's ever tried anything like this before. It's got to be Emilio Delgado."

Giving the dagger another flip, Damon received the news impassively.

Graham grinned. "Something tells me you don't agree."

Damon laid the dagger on the desk, settled his elbows on the cushioned leather armrests of his chair, and steepled his fingers beneath his chin. "Stealing one of my arms shipments is just not Delgado's style. It's too subtle."

"But he was desperate to get those arms for the Rayos."

"Yes, but remember, he didn't know I would refuse until last night. He's not the type to have a contingency plan waiting to put into action. He reacts to the circumstances of the moment. And once I said no, he didn't have enough time to make the kind of detailed plan necessary for hijacking a large shipment of arms."

"He tried to have you killed, Damon."

"Again, a reaction of the moment. It was poorly planned and executed, was it not? Knowing Delgado, he made grandiose promises to the Rayos based on his belief that he could manipulate me, and he was banking on the success of this arms buy to build credibility with other groups. Now he's lost face, and he's thinking that if he eliminates me, he'll regain that face and have a clear field. He'll try to kill me again with a better-planned attempt."

"We'll be ready, don't worry," Graham responded, steel determination in his voice.

"It's not Delgado who worries me." Damon

thoughtfully rubbed his finger down the outer slope of his eyebrow.

"Nevertheless, I intend to keep an eye on him."

"Do that." Damon threw a glance at his watch, pushed away from his desk, and stood. "In the meantime . . ."

"Ah, yes, the young woman with the pearls. I heard she was still aboard. How long is she going to be with us?"

"It depends."

"Tell me something. Is it the woman or the pearls?"

At the door Damon turned and smiled at Graham. "Keep me abreast of any new developments."

"I appreciate your coming for me, Benes," Alex said to the small wiry man walking along beside her, "but I'm sure I could have found my way."

"I am happy to be of service. The yacht is quite large, and Mr. Barand would be most put out with me if I allowed you to become lost."

Through the formality of his words, Alex caught a humorous note. "Your accent sounds European, Benes, but I can't quite place it."

"Eastern European," he said proudly. "I am from Czechoslovakia, the same as Mr. Barand."

"I didn't know Damon was from Czechoslovakia."

"Yes, Miss Sheldon, although I believe he has been away for some time and is no longer a citizen."

"I wonder why?"

"You must understand that there is an oppressive spirit over our land," he said earnestly, "and sometimes being a citizen of another country is more convenient."

Before she could respond, Benes opened a door and ushered her into the grand salon where Damon was waiting. All questions fled her mind at the sight of him. He was standing with a bank of windows at his back, his tall, lean body outlined by a light that reflected with soft brightness off the blue sea. He held out his hand, and she crossed the room and went into his arms. A faint smile hovered on his lips as he stared down at her. "Thank you, Benes."

"Yes, sir."

The door closed with a discreet click, and Damon bent his head and kissed her slowly, deeply. "Are you hungry?"

"No. Yes." She laughed, distracted by the kiss. "I'm not sure."

"You should eat. The chefs have prepared a little something."

She glanced over her shoulder at a table arrayed with at least fifty separate dishes. "A little something?"

"I have two chefs who do nothing but cook for me and my guests. They get bored if they have nothing to do."

"I've always considered boredom a great sin," she said solemnly, but her warm brown eyes twinkled with laughter.

His smile broadened. "Ah, Alexandra, what am I to do with you?"

It was a leading question, she decided, and one best left unanswered.

He surveyed her aqua halter-necked sundress. "Where are your pearls?"

"Put away in a case in my luggage."

"Perhaps you'd like to put them in my vault."

She grinned. "If one of your employees did happen to work up the courage to deliberately go against you and steal them, where would he take them?"

His shrug conveyed nonchalance. "You're right, of course. Your necklace is quite safe on the ship. I just thought that if the pearls were in my vault, you'd have an even greater measure of peace of mind. But if you're satisfied . . . Will you wear them tonight?"

It was the intonation she thought she heard rather than the words themselves that disturbed her on some subconscious level. But the meaning remained elusive, and she decided she was being silly. "If you like."

He nodded, then waved toward the table. "What looks good to you?"

"Actually, nothing. I never eat until I've been up a few hours. What I'd really like to do is go outside and see where we're going. Where *are* we going, by the way?"

He chuckled. "This morning, before we weighed anchor, was the time to ask, Alex. I could be taking you into the Bermuda triangle for all you know."

"I'd go gladly as long as you were with me."

He stopped dead still, and his eyes narrowed. "Why have you remained a virgin for so long?"

She shrugged. "I guess I was waiting for you."

"God, Alex," he muttered, "what *am* I going to do with you?"

He had asked her that question before, Damon reflected, but in reality he wanted no answer. Her answers tended to burrow their way beneath his skin, irritating him, intriguing him, making him want her. He pulled her back into his arms for a quick fierce kiss.

"It's exhilarating, isn't it?" she asked a short time later, standing by Damon's side on the topmost deck of the *Ares*. "The speed is incredible."

"We're cruising at about twenty-two knots, but we're not by any means at top speed."

She pushed her hair away from her face and sent him a deliberately provocative look. "And to *where* exactly are we cruising?"

With a grin he pointed toward the bow. "That way."

"Great. I've always wanted to go to *that way*."

He laughed and dropped a kiss on her mouth. Last night she had waited with breathless anticipation for their first kiss, she thought, and now he seemed to be kissing her all the time.

She buried her face against his throat and drew the heady smell of his potent masculinity into her senses, then she rested her cheek against his chest and scanned the unlimited vista of blue sea and sky before them. "Oh, look, Damon." She straightened and pointed at the sky. "There's a dragon."

"I've sailed these waters many times, but I've never seen a dragon in the sky."

Her head whipped around at the amusement in his voice, and she saw that his eyes were on her instead of on the sky. "That's because you've never looked." She took his face in her hands and turned it up to the sky. "Look!"

"That's a cloud."

"It all depends on how you view it." Laughing in humorous despair, she pointed out the form of the dragon. "See, there's the long tail, it's kind of jagged, and there's the head with the mouth open. Look, you can even see a little stream of fire."

"A little stream of fire?" he asked teasingly.

"Damon, *study* the cloud."

"I'd rather study you," he said, his gaze intent on her. Damn, but she was watchable, he thought. Her face was a constantly changing pattern of expressions and emotions that was beautiful and entrancing to watch.

"I guess I can't object too much to that."

His fingers attempted to comb order into her windblown hair. "Why don't I show you the ship? There's a cinema, a tape library, a library, a swimming pool, a gym, a sauna, a game room, a massage room, a—"

Her laughter interrupted him. "And here I was afraid I might be bored."

"Liar," he whispered before he kissed her again.

• • •

Damon couldn't concentrate on the movie playing on the giant screen before him. Sitting beside Alex in the darkness of his private suede-upholstered viewing room, he frowned up at the images of the movie's two leading characters. Usually he managed to find some amusement and escape in the movies he had delivered aboard the *Ares,* even if it was only in the pleasure he received from picking apart the plot line.

This movie had just been released in the States to rave reviews and had come highly recommended. But he was finding that Alex was occupying his attention, and he didn't understand why. She wasn't talking, fidgeting, or even sitting that close to him. Still, he couldn't get his mind off her.

It had been a definite surprise to him when she had asked for her own stateroom. Normally sex was the one and only reason he kept a woman aboard, and he would have put any woman ashore at the first mention of a separate stateroom.

But Alex had something no other woman in the world had—the Pearls of Sharah. He was determined to possess the necklace, and, he decided firmly, it shouldn't take him too long to figure out how.

He didn't need to take Alex to his bed, because once he had the fabulous necklace for his very own, he would be satisfied. With the decision made, he immediately felt better.

He reached for her hand and idly played with her long, slender fingers. They were sensitive and strong, he thought. On a man's skin they would tantalize and pleasure. He lifted her hand and kissed each fingertip.

Warmth shivered through Alex. Out of the corner of her eye, she saw that Damon's attention was on the screen. But as she watched him, his lips parted slightly and his tongue came out to lick the pad of one of her fingers. She caught her bottom lip between her teeth in an effort to stem her heated reaction.

He turned his head toward her. "Don't you like the movie?"

She swallowed against a suddenly dry throat. "I'm having a hard time following the story line."

"It's very simple. It's a love story set to a background of danger and suspense."

"I got that much," she whispered.

The man on the screen stared deeply into the woman's eyes, and Damon wondered what had happened to the villain who had been chasing the man and woman. *He needed to keep his mind on the film.* He jerked her fingers away from his mouth and laid her hand on his thigh. The movie couldn't be as bad as he thought it was, he decided, then put his arm around Alex and drew her closer until he could feel her warmth against him.

Onscreen the man unbuttoned the woman's blouse and pushed the garment off her shoulders, then he brought up his hands and covered the lacy fabric of her bra. The woman threw back her head and shut her eyes in ecstasy.

Damon's hand smoothed over Alex's shoulder.

She was wearing full-cut shorts that hit her legs about mid-thigh, and a halter top that left her midriff, shoulders, and back bare.

Alex took a deep breath. Watching movie love scenes with a date beside her was nothing new, of course, but she and her dates had always been in packed movie theaters. She and Damon were completely alone, lounging more than sitting, on a plushly cushioned couch in a private screening room. The situation was ripe for all sorts of things, and much to her dismay, the prospect excited her.

"Darling," the woman on the screen said.

Damon slipped his hand under the halter strap, and soft, satiny skin greeted his fingers.

The man on the screen pulled the woman to him and pressed his lips to her shoulder, then brought his mouth to her parted lips. The kiss was hard and wild, and soon the woman's bra was off.

Alex shifted on the couch and felt Damon's muscled thigh flex beneath her hand. His long fingers smoothed down to the top of her breast and rubbed across the soft fullness.

The screen couple sank onto the bed, the man on top of the woman. His hand ran up her leg and disappeared beneath her skirt. The music swelled and mingled with the greedy, desire-filled sounds made by the couple.

Involuntarily Damon conjured up a picture of what Alex would look like with her breasts bared and him on top of her. His fingers found her nipple beneath her halter and worked the crest until it hardened. Briefly he closed his eyes as the urge to take the enticing peak into his mouth washed over him.

Alex lay her head back against his arm, suffused with heat. If she told him to stop, he would. So why didn't she, she wondered. The answer came easily. Because she loved the intimacy. Because his touch felt so good. And because, dammit, she just plain didn't want him to stop.

The characters on the screen began to simulate lovemaking, but what Alex was feeling was not make-believe. Sensations in her spiraled higher. The movie couple reached a loudly satisfying drawn-out climax. Alex rolled her head along Damon's arm and met his eyes. She could see in the light from the screen that they were hungry and hot. With a groan she buried her face in his shoulder, and the motion wrenched his hand from her breast.

Quiet reigned on the screen. Quiet reigned in the *Ares*'s screening room.

Held in Damon's embrace, Alex waited for her pulse to slow. "I feel so foolish," she whispered.

He angled her face up so he could see her expression. "Why?"

"Because just last night I told you that I wanted time to catch my breath. And then I let something like this happen."

He drew a deep, ragged breath. "Don't be upset. Not that much happened, and nothing will until you're ready."

She cringed slightly. It had taken very little time for her to become so used to his kisses that now she craved them. Would she covet his touch with the same speed? Almost as if in answer, she felt her nipples throb. "Maybe not that much happened by your definition."

Damon silently cursed himself. Why in the hell had he let himself touch her like that? He could have scared her off. Hadn't he just told himself he didn't need to take her to bed? Then, why, he wondered angrily, was he experiencing a painful swelling in his loins? He lightly traced his fingertips along her jaw. "Perhaps we should watch another movie?"

"How about *Snow White and the Seven Dwarfs*?"

He threw back his head and laughed. "Go get into your bathing suit. We'll cool off in the pool."

Lying on a double lounger by the pool with Damon beside her, Alex sighed with pleasure. "This Mediterranean sun makes me feel as though I don't have a bone in my body."

He pushed his sunglasses up on his head and gave her bikini-clad body a clinical survey. "With your fair skin you need to be careful. The sun's stronger than it feels." He poured out a handful of suntan lotion and rubbed it down one of her legs.

Breathlessness interfered with her contentment. "Do you provide this service for all your guests?"

"Only for those with skin as touchable as yours," he said. He grimly acknowledged to himself the truth of his remark and switched his attention to her other leg. When he reached her upper thigh, his hand slowed and lingered against his will. When his assistant approached, Damon practically barked at him. "What is it, Graham?"

Glad for the intrusion, Alex shielded her eyes and smiled at the blond-haired man she had met and talked with the day after the *Ares* had sailed from St. Tropez. "Hi, Graham."

"Hi, Alex, and thank you. At least I can always count on you for a civil greeting." He nodded toward the swimming pool. "How was the water?"

"Great. You should have come in with us."

"I have a workaholic for a boss." He cast an amused glance at Damon. "Or, at least, he usually is."

She grinned. "I don't understand how anyone could be a workaholic on this ship, surrounded by so much beauty."

"I know what you mean. This is a far cry from the small town in Minnesota where I grew up."

"Minnesota? Really? That's a lovely state. Did you go to college there also?"

He nodded. "The University of Minnesota. Great school. After I graduated I went into the army. Unfortunately since then I've been able to get back only a few times. My folks and I usually meet somewhere in between the place where I am at the time of their vacation and Minnesota."

"They get a nice holiday that way."

"They seem to enjoy it."

Damon listened to the exchange with growing

irritation. "Was there something you wanted, Graham?"

"What? Oh, yes." He extended a leather folder toward Damon. "I need your okay before I send these out."

Damon set aside the lotion, opened the folder, then did a quick scan of the papers. "They're fine."

Taking back the folder from Damon, Graham grinned at her. "I guess I'll see you later. Don't get too much sun."

She lifted her hand in a wave. "And don't work too hard." When Graham had gone, Alex turned to face Damon. "Why were you so short with him?"

"Because he was looking at you like you were a piece of delicious chocolate and he was a chocolate addict."

"You're exaggerating."

"No, I'm not." He handed her the bottle of suntan lotion. "Here, put some of this on your arms and chest."

Damon settled back onto the lounger and shut his eyes, considering. Had he been *jealous*? It was a displeasing idea. Emotions such as jealousy could be dangerous; they coiled and tangled in your mind and kept you from thinking straight. He'd have to be more careful.

Fortunately Alex couldn't have that much more time left on her vacation.

"You're not putting enough lotion on, Alex." He took the bottle from her and poured the rich liquid into his hand and smoothed it over her throat and chest. Her skin was sun-warmed, and a couple of times his fingers strayed beneath the bikini top.

The first time it happened he considered it an accident.

The second time he considered it carelessness on his part.

The third time he didn't consider at all.

He delved beneath the skimpy top and took all of her into his hand with a pressure that strained, then unbound the knot that held the top together.

Alex ran her hand to the back of his neck and brought his mouth to hers, and he kissed her with a passion that if it were out of control might have bothered him. But all he wanted to do, he told himself, was touch her. And kiss her. And so he did. Until he had to dive into the cool water of the pool and swim innumerable laps to release his tension.

Damon turned as Alex came into his stateroom, and in the silence of the room he heard the whisper of her gold silk dress as it fluttered around her legs. The dress swept off her shoulders and draped over her body in a sinuous spill of softness and made a perfect background for the pearls.

She'd been aboard the *Ares* for three days now, and his desire for her continued to astound and confound him.

"We're eating in here?" she asked.

He nodded, giving a cursory glance at the round

pink marble table where Benes had laid out their midnight supper. "I thought it would be nice, but if you'd rather eat someplace else . . ."

The strain of Damon's constant kisses and touches had begun to tell on Alex. She wasn't sure she would ever catch her breath around this man. And now she wasn't so sure she wanted to. The idea of eating in his bedroom was a dangerous one, but then, she supposed the sensuous surroundings couldn't be that much more perilous to her constantly inflamed senses than the screening room, or the pool, or any of the decks and salons in which they'd kissed and touched over the last few days.

She crossed to him and went into his arms. "It doesn't matter. Since I've been with you, food, or where I eat it, is the last thing I think about."

He enclosed her in his embrace and pressed his mouth to her throat, right above the pearls. He must be cautious, he told himself as he licked her skin and savored the sweetness. She had a way of making ingenious remarks when he least expected them, and it brought him to the point of instant, aching arousal. Nothing but iron will on several occasions today had kept him from taking her. With her his blood ran much too hot. Only the knowledge that she would be leaving soon to go back to her home in Connecticut made this uncharacteristically intense desire he felt for her acceptable.

He gazed down at her. "I have a surprise for you."

Delight spread across her face. "What?"

"Just wait." He seated her at the table, then walked to the bed. An ingenious combination of carved obsidian and oyster-hued crushed taffeta made up the headboard.

A press of a hidden button disclosed a control panel. With a press of another button Alex heard a faint sound above her. Tilting her head back, she looked up to see the ceiling slowly sliding open. As a black velvet star-studded sky was revealed, her lips parted in silent wonder.

He joined her at the table, his mouth twisted in a satisfied smile. "I thought you might enjoy dining alfresco."

"That's amazing. Did you design it yourself?"

"Of course. I always like to leave myself a way to escape."

Damon trapped was an image too painful to contemplate, so she deliberately took the conversation in a different direction. "It also gives you a magnificent view of the heavens."

"I suppose it does." He snapped his napkin open, and his eyes settled on her pearls. Tonight she had simply hung them around her neck with the clasp at the back beneath her hair. "You know, you shouldn't be traveling with those pearls."

"Why not? I enjoy wearing them."

"I know you do, but they're very valuable. There are jewel thieves all over Europe who would love to get their hands on them. You should at least have a guard with you."

She wrinkled her nose distastefully. "That would take the pleasure out of wearing them."

"You're probably right, but a piece of jewelry like your necklace is a responsibility." Damon paused. He was about to be abrupt and tactless, but the need to get Alex out of his life was becoming more important by the hour. "I'd still like to buy the pearls from you. I'll give you any amount of money you ask."

She went still. "You really want them, don't you?"

"Yes."

"Damon, my answer is, and will always be, no. Please don't ask me again."

"Very well." He reached for the wine bottle. "This is an excellent vintage. I think you'll enjoy it."

While he poured the wine, she studied him. There was no sign that he was upset over her refusal, but a thread of disquiet played in her mind.

"By the way," he said, "I've just received word that a Ying Ch'ing porcelain from the Sung Dynasty has become available. There'll be someone bringing it aboard soon for my inspection." He frowned. "The problem is, this man who'll be trying to sell it to me has brought me defective pieces before. I won't buy a piece that's flawed."

Unconsciously she touched the scar at her jaw. "But you're talking about something that's centuries old. How can it be without flaws? Besides, the beauty of a piece doesn't depend on perfection."

"Your necklace is perfect."

Why did he have to keep focusing on the pearls? "I haven't had an expert look at it. Maybe it is, and maybe it isn't. It doesn't matter. Beauty is made up of all sorts of different components. Look at the Acropolis. Every year more of it disintegrates. But you don't see ruin when you look at it. Instead, you feel the richness of its history and the strength of the belief of the people who built it and who walked along its ancient halls. I can't believe that if the impossible happened and the Acropolis went up for sale, you wouldn't buy it."

He felt equal parts fascination, bafflement, and annoyance, because he knew that if tonight he went and stood before the Acropolis, he would not see any of those things she mentioned. "I wouldn't buy it." He took a sip of wine, and his lips indented with a dry smile. "It wouldn't fit on the *Ares*."

"And you're still not going to buy the vase if it's flawed, are you?"

"No." He studied her and his expression turned thoughtful. "You touched your scar a moment ago."

"Did I?" She shrugged. "After all this time I'm not even aware of it." Had he ever touched her scar, she wondered.

"What happened?"

Her eyes clouded as she remembered. "It was an automobile accident. My father was driving. Another car hit us head-on. It was a long time ago, before safety glass, and I went straight through the windshield; my whole face was lacerated and embedded with glass. My father was killed."

To his consternation, he felt a tug of pain at her sorrow. He knew what it was like to lose a parent at a young age, but, bewilderingly, his sensitivity toward her seemed to go beyond that knowledge.

"My father and I were very close, and I was devastated by his death."

"But you still had your mother." He had lost both parents.

"Yes. She arrived at the hospital, saw my face, and refused to look at me again."

"Don't you think that was natural under the circumstances?"

"No. There wasn't anything natural about it. Her concern wasn't that I was hurt, but that I was ugly. You see, she was a very beautiful woman, and she couldn't stand having a daughter who wasn't in her image. Somehow, frightened and upset as I was, I sensed this. Emotionally I completely closed up. The only person who could reach me was my grandmother, and she took over the raising of me, thank God."

"You obviously had most of your scars repaired."

To his surprise, she laughed. "For years I refused all surgery. Gradually my grandmother got me to see that I was doing it out of spite for my mother." She shook her head in amused reflection. "Lord, I was a stubborn child. Finally, though, I agreed to a series of operations, until at last all that was left was this." She fingered the scar. "I decided it wasn't worth putting myself through another ordeal."

"You were right."

The scar on her face. Flaws in things of beauty. Suddenly Alex didn't want to talk about either of them anymore. She wasn't beautiful, and, at least in his eyes, she would be flawed. *So what,* she asked herself defiantly. She had been aware right from the first what she was risking by becoming involved with the enigmatic Damon Barand, who chose to surround himself with danger and the deep, fathomless sea. But she strongly believed that the things she would lose if she didn't allow this relationship a chance to flourish and bloom were immeasurable.

The sea murmured around them. The sky blazed with silver-starred magic above them. If ever there was a night meant for love, she thought, it was this one. Staring into Damon's black eyes, she saw a velvet, heated softness that made her go weak.

For a moment it seemed as if time were suspended, and the night held its breath.

Then a light knock on the door made them jump.

Damon was the first to recover. "Come in."

Benes rolled in the dinner cart and began serving them.

"We'll be dropping anchor off Corsica sometime this evening," Damon said, filling the uncomfortable gap of silence that had fallen between them. "I thought you might enjoy exploring Calvi. It's not the height of the tourist season yet, so it shouldn't be too crowded, and you might find the citadel interesting. I'll send someone along with you who can act as guide."

"What do you mean, send someone? Aren't you coming with me?"

He shook his head. "A business associate will be coptering aboard. I'll be tied up most of the day, I'm afraid."

Covering her disappointment, Alex smiled at Benes. "May I have a cup of coffee please?"

At three o'clock in the morning, in the *Ares's* NASA-style communications center, Damon eyed Graham steadily. "Tell me."

"It was a well-planned, well-executed attack. We lost six men and the entire arms shipment."

"Damn!"

"That's twice in a matter of days. It's an unheard of action. It has to be Delgado."

Damon shook his head, disturbed. "There's something strange going on here. I just can't put my finger on it. But I'm almost sure that it's not Delgado."

"Almost sure? Damon, we've got to do something. We can't sit back and wait until the next shipment is hijacked. There's too much at stake."

"We have a shipment starting for Nicaragua tonight, don't we?"

"Yes."

Damon nodded, pondering.

Graham pushed his fingers impatiently through his hair. "I think we need to hit Delgado *now* and save that shipment."

"We wait." Turning his back on Graham, Damon walked to the window and stared out at the dark sea and the distant lights of Corsica. Somewhere out there someone was working to bring him down. Who was it? Why was this person doing it?

He had that feeling again, the one that always raised the hairs on his skin. Except this time he had the oddest sensation that what was about to happen was not unexpected. *What was it?*

When Damon awoke the next morning, sunlight was streaming through the opening in his stateroom's ceiling.

And the eerie feeling he had had the night before was still with him.

He rose quickly, dressed, and went to look for Alex.

She was gone.

Four

On the end of the Quai Landry at the base of the citadel, Alex put her shopping bag down and consulted her guidebook. According to the book, the Tour du Sel, the massive round tower that stood before her, had been built in the fifteenth century and had been used for storing salt. A *lot* of salt, she thought, raising her hand to shield her eyes from the sun. But she still couldn't quite see. . . . She took a few steps backward and bumped into something tall and solid, and a sharp pain stabbed through the center of her back.

"Oh, I'm sorry," she exclaimed as hands steadied her. Turning, she discovered that she had collided with a nice-looking dark-haired man in his late thirties. "I mean"—she quickly searched her mind for the French—"tous mes regrets."

The man laughed pleasantly. "There's nothing

to apologize for. I'm afraid I wasn't looking where I was going either."

She relaxed and eyed him with friendly interest. He was dressed casually in an open-necked shirt and chinos and was obviously out for a day of sight-seeing as she was. His round thin-rimmed glasses gave his strong face an intellectual air. "Thank goodness you speak English. My school French has been strained to the limits today."

"I know what you mean." He picked up his camera, hanging by a strap from around his neck, and gave it a quick check.

She rubbed the spot in the middle of her back. "I hit your camera, didn't I? I hope I didn't damage it, but if I did, I'll be glad to pay for any repairs."

"The camera looks fine." He gave her a reassuring smile, then glanced at her shopping bags. "I see you've already visited the shops. Have you been to the citadel yet?"

"I did that first thing, and I loved it. Have you been in the cathedral of St. John the Baptist?"

He shook his head regretfully. "I missed that."

"Oh, you must go back. In the small chapel to the left of the choir stall, there's a sixteenth-century carved wooden Madonna from Seville that's extraordinary. Her face is so serene, yet I could actually see pain in her eyes. And"—she rushed on in her enthusiasm—"in the chapel to the right, there's an ebony crucifix that was carried around the ramparts of the citadel during the siege of Calvi by—" Suddenly she broke off and laughed at herself. "You have to understand, I'm very impressed by anything that has endured as long as the citadel. I'm an American, and our history is so short."

His eyebrows rose over the top rim of his glasses and his eyes twinkled. "You know, I would never have guessed you were an American."

She made a face. "Sticks out, does it?"

"Americans are the friendliest people on earth, very open. You people are wonderful because there's nothing blasé about you."

She eyed him curiously. "Then you aren't American?" He had a slight accent, but he could still be a U.S. citizen.

"No," he said without elaboration. "I was just about to have something to eat. Please join me."

She glanced uncertainly at her watch, trying to remember when Benes had said he would send the speedboat for her. "I don't know. I think I should be getting back."

"Back?"

She didn't want to tell him about Damon or the *Ares*, because all day long she'd been trying to understand why the sensually charged air between them had dissolved so suddenly last night. When Benes brought in their dinner, Damon seemed to withdraw from her. Shortly after they finished eating, he had asked to be excused, citing work that needed to be done. "Back to where I'm staying," she said, and hoped he wouldn't ask her where that was. He didn't.

"Surely you can spare another thirty minutes. I

happen to know that the first little café along the Quai Landry serves the best *imbrocciatta*." At her dubious look, he grinned. "Fritters made with a kind of cream cheese in the batter and flavored with brandy. You can't leave Calvi without trying them."

It did sound good, she decided. Damon would probably still be busy with his business associate. Turning her head, she scanned Calvi's harbor, where a number of pleasure boats rode. But because of the *Ares*'s size, the ship had anchored outside the harbor and couldn't be seen from this point on the quay. She made her decision quickly. "I'd love to try the dish. By the way, my name is Alex."

"Alex, I'm Kito." He bent and lifted her shopping bag. "Let me carry this for you. It feels like you bought out quite a few of the shops."

She laughed and fell into step beside him. "Almost."

An hour later Kito smilingly returned Alex's wave of good-bye and watched as she hurried down the quay, her short, swinging skirt showing off her long, well-shaped legs to their best advantage and causing more than one male head to turn. His gaze followed her until she disappeared from view, then he settled back in his chair. Raising his wineglass, he studied the lovely deep red color. Slowly his lips compressed with a hint of hard cruelty.

•   •   •

Alex saw Damon before he saw her. He was standing on the dock talking with two men, each of whom carried walkie-talkies. "Damon," she called out, and moved quickly toward him.

He heard his name, and his head jerked around.

"Did your meeting finish early?" she asked, stepping onto the dock.

He took hold of one of her arms and yanked her to him, causing her to drop the shopping bag. "Where have you been?"

"Touring Calvi," she said, puzzled. "What's wrong? You knew where I was going. We talked about it yesterday, remember?"

"Yes, I remember." His words were forced out from between clenched teeth. His body was tensed, his face taut. "Do *you* remember when I said I'd send someone along to act as guide?"

"I didn't need a guide. Damon, you're hurting my arm."

He relaxed his grip and rubbed the red marks his fingers had made. "I'm sorry. It's just that I was worried about you."

"Why? What on earth is wrong?"

"I've had this feeling . . ." He shook his head as if to clear it. "Something could have happened to you."

"Well, nothing happened, and I've had a wonderful time."

"Good. That's good." He sent a brief nod to one of his men, who spoke rapidly into his walkie-talkie, then jumped into one of the two speedboats from the *Ares* that were tied up at the dock, and started it. "By the way," Damon said casually, "Benes said that he brought you ashore?"

"Yes. I hope I didn't get him in trouble, but I didn't want to bother you."

"Next time bother me." He pressed a quick, hard kiss to her mouth. When he lifted his head, he muttered, "Let's go."

"Wait, my shopping bag."

"I'll get it." Damon grabbed up the bag with a jerk.

"Wait till you see what I bought," Alex said, peering into the shopping bag. "I found some really great things."

Damon's impatient frown clearly showed his attitude about souvenirs. "You're a wealthy young woman, Alex. You could buy something of real beauty and value. I can't understand why you'd want to waste your money on that junk."

He spoke sharply, still very much on edge, even though he had her back in her stateroom, safe and sound. But he remembered the anxiety he had felt when he had discovered that she had gone ashore without a bodyguard. Every nerve in his body had gone on the alert.

Suddenly things were happening he didn't understand and couldn't seem to control—feelings that wouldn't go away; and arms shipments that never arrived at their destinations, taken by people who came out of nowhere and disappeared into nowhere.

Alex considered Damon's dark mood thoughtfully. Something was going on about which she knew nothing. She didn't like his shutting her out like this. But while she was close to the point of admitting to herself that she loved him, she knew he did not return her feelings. She was hopeful that time would bring his love to her, but in the meantime she wasn't sure she had a right to pry.

"These things may not have much value, but they're quite beautiful in their own way. Come look. For instance . . ." She pulled several pieces of embroidery from the bag. "I bought these from the elderly woman who'd done all this fine work. Look at the exquisite detail and lovely colors. I can't begin to guess how much time it must have taken for her to do it. And her hands were so gnarled, but when I left, she was sitting out in the afternoon sun, working on another piece as if she couldn't imagine doing anything else."

She handed one of the pieces to Damon. He gave it a cursory glance then tossed it onto the bed. "But what are you going to do with all this stuff?"

"I'm not sure. Perhaps I'll frame them, or make throw pillows out of them, and then every time I look at the embroidery, I'll remember my day in Calvi." She brought out two small woven baskets and held them up to him. He nodded abruptly.

Suddenly she tired of trying to get him out of

his strange temper. "Damon, what is bothering you?"

"Nothing. What else did you buy?"

Half angry, she retrieved the last item from her bag, a small picture of the citadel, imaginatively done in bits and pieces of wood. "This type of work is called *art galtique*. Some of the pictures are done in pebbles, but I liked the wood."

"Really?" he asked, not caring in the least.

"Yes, and I guess that's it." She threw a last look into the shopping bag. "Wait a minute. What's this?"

He had been about to turn away, but the surprise in her voice caught his attention. "What?"

She delved deeply into the bag, brought out a small gold cross that dangled from a thin gold chain, and held it up for him to see.

Damon reached out, took the necklace, and twined the golden chain about his fingers until he had the cross in his hand. As if in a trance, he stared at the cross. And slowly his blood turned cold.

"Did you talk to anyone while you were in Calvi?" he asked hoarsely.

"I talked to a lot of people. Damon, what's wrong? You've gone pale. Are you all right?"

He tore his gaze away from the cross and looked at her. "Tell me who you talked to."

"I don't understand—"

"Tell me, Alex! It's important."

"Well, shopkeepers, uh, some fellow tourists,

oh, and then there were some children who were playing—"

"The tourists. Was there a tall, dark-haired man about my age?"

"Yes. I had a glass of wine and something called *imbrocciatta* with him."

"What was his name?"

"I don't know his last name, but his first name was Kito. What does he have to do with the cross? And why was it in my shopping bag?"

He closed his hand into a fist, barely noticing the sharp points of the cross cutting into the flesh of his palm.

Kito.

Now he understood. Now he knew. Kito was the what and the who behind his premonitory feeling about the hijacking of his arms, his concern over Alex.

For years, deep beneath the surface of his conscious thought, he had expected—in fact, been waiting for—this moment.

He turned on his heel and headed for the door.

"Damon, wait? What is it?"

He was already halfway out the door when he heard the alarm in her voice. He paused, took a deep, calming breath, and turned back. "I'm sorry, Alex. There's something I need to take care of. I'll be back in a little while."

"But I don't understand. Who was that man I met today?"

His jaw tightened. "Someone I used to know a long time ago."

"But why did he put the cross in my bag?"

"It's nothing for you to worry about. It was just his rather convoluted way of sending me a message."

"You mean the cross has some sort of special meaning?"

The imprint of the cross dug into his palm. He relaxed his hand. "Please stop worrying. Why don't you rest for a while, and I'll meet you in the grand salon in two hours." With a wave of his hand he left the room.

Alex sank onto the bed and stared after him.

Damon absently stroked the downward slope of his eyebrow as he studied the papers in his lap. His dark brown rough-linen pants were zipped but not fastened; his feet were bare; and the warm beige shirt he had chosen for the evening hung open over his chest. When the knock came at the door of his stateroom, he called, "Come in."

Alex entered, her teal and turquoise silk strapless dress swirling around her, the pearls a dazzling addition to her appearance.

Surprised that Alex had come to his stateroom, Damon set aside the papers and studied her. She was clearly in a state of agitation, but the vibrancy that had made Graham pick her out of the party crowd still radiated from her, making her incredibly desirable.

For the first time Damon acknowledged to himself that in her own way, Alex was as much a problem to him as Kito.

Slowly he rose from the chair. "You're early. Is there something wrong?"

Alex's already-disturbed nerves jumped at the sexy sight Damon made, half dressed for the evening, and she laced her hands together. "I want you to tell me what all that was about this afternoon."

"I thought I did." He crossed the room and kissed her cheek. "You look very lovely tonight."

She jerked away from him, knowing that physical contact with him would break all chain of thought. "Answer me, Damon. I've been thinking about this ever since you left my room. When I first realized something was bothering you, I decided I didn't have a right to pry. But I was *used* this afternoon, and I think I deserve an explanation."

He extended his arms, intending to comfort, but she deliberately moved out of his reach. His arms dropped to his side, and he clenched his fist. He could not remember ever trying to offer a woman only comfort, and Alex had just pulled away from him twice.

"Damon, I sat at an outdoor café for over an hour, chatting and comparing notes on Calvi with a man I believed to be nothing more than a fellow tourist. I feel like a fool, and I want to know what he was up to."

He took his time, choosing his words carefully. "His full name is Kito Sobota. He and I grew up together in Czechoslovakia. Our families lived next door to each other."

"You mean you were boyhood friends?" she asked incredulously.

He ran his hand around the back of his neck with impatience. "I told you earlier he was someone I knew a long time ago."

"Then why all the intrigue?"

"Alex . . ." The answers she wanted lay too close to the bone. Unable to tell her the whole story, he tried to gloss over the matter. "It's just Kito's way."

The fact that she was making him angry mattered little to Alex. There was a puzzle here with too many of the pieces missing for her to come up with a solution. But if she ever got all the pieces together, she had a feeling she would know Damon. She waited, and when he didn't volunteer anything more, she said, "So what you're asking me to believe is that he wanted to surprise you, to send you some sort of message?"

He ground his teeth together. "It's the *truth*. I'll just have to wait and see what he wants."

"When was the last time you saw him?"

"It's been years."

Alex shook her head uncomprehendingly. "You're not really telling me anything. Why didn't he come to you in person?"

"Because he hates me. Alex, let it drop."

She stared at him in surprise. "Hates you?"

"Dammit, I said, *let it drop.*" He gave an exasperated sigh, but the exasperation was at himself. Ghosts from his past were upsetting him more than he would have thought possible, and he was taking it out on Alex. "What can I say. I'm sorry. You're right. You were used, and for that I can only apologize. All I can do is make damned sure it won't happen again."

"No, Damon, that's not all you can do. You can tell me about the cross."

His expression changed, closed, became cold. "I've told you all I can."

"You mean all you *will*. Damon, the expression on your face while you looked at that cross was frightening."

He half turned away. "You're imagining things."

She knew she wasn't. Angry, discouraged, she spoke before she thought. "Maybe I should leave."

He looked back at her, his eyes narrowing. "Is that what you want?"

The question stopped her. She was sure she loved Damon Barand, even with all his complexities and dark secrets. The love had started at her first sight of him that electric night on the Côte d'Azur and had grown steadily ever since. He had given her time as she had requested, but she still felt this wonderful and amazing breathless quality every time she was with him.

Loving this man was not wise. Danger surrounded him and emanated from him. If she could avoid the danger, she certainly would, but to get the man, she believed she might have to accept the danger. Charlotte had taught her that the things one regretted most in life were not the things one did but the things one didn't do.

Suddenly she needed no more time. She had made her decision, and it was irreversible.

She moved until she was standing in front of him. "No, I don't want to leave."

He barely heard her whispered words, but he saw her reach behind her and unzip her dress. The teal and turquoise silk fell away, and she quickly pushed it down past her hips to the floor and stepped out of it.

His need for her hit him full force. For days he had been denying the importance of having her. But now all his denials came apart like a wave crashing against rocky cliffs and shattering into sea mist. She was offering herself to him, and he had to take.

When she raised her arms to unwind the pearls from around her neck, he stopped her, saying, "No. Leave the pearls on."

Wearing only the rope of pearls and a narrow band of ivory lace panties, she met his gaze. His breath caught in his throat. With every look and gesture she made, with every word she spoke, his desire for her had steadily grown, and he was already hard with need. He peeled off his shirt and tossed it carelessly over a chair. Then he lifted her into his arms and carried her to the bed.

She heard his soft, even breathing in the stillness around them, and she suddenly realized that the stateroom was completely soundproof. They were sealed together in a sensually textured world of twilight colors where the only sounds would be the ones they made.

They lay down together and pushed back the satin comforter. When the last of their clothing had disappeared, he leaned over her and brushed his thumb across her bottom lip. "So soft." He dipped his head, took the fullness gently between his teeth, and played with it. He was aching for her, but he never rushed. "So sweet. Talk to me, Alexandra. Tell me what you want."

"I want you."

The hand he ran over her silky skin shook slightly. Her auburn hair spread in wild splendor over the oyster satin sheets like spilled liquid fire. The pearls fell over her fair skin and down her slender strong-limbed body in a glowing, sinuous pattern. Her warm brown eyes met his with trust and with an innocent passion. It had been a long time since he had felt guilt over anything. His world was too filled with absolutes to allow such a troubling emotion. But for one brief moment he wondered if he should send her on her way before . . .

She lifted her head off the bed and touched his mouth with hers. "I want you," she said again.

The fires inside him raged higher, the flames eating away at the tight reins he held over his emotions. "Damn," he muttered raggedly. "You have such a way about you."

With his mouth, his tongue, and his hands, he set about learning her. It amazed him that as many women as he had had, Alex still managed to surprise him. The instinctive way she kissed him, the gentle, seductive way she touched him, the unrestrained way she reacted to his hands on her body, were vividly different from the learned responses he normally received from women. Heightened impressions and dizzying excitement spiraled through him, making him feel as though he were freefalling through air made up entirely of Alex.

His tongue traced along her stomach, and the clenching of his muscles told him he'd never taken quite this path before. Inflamed, his mouth closed over her nipple, and the taste he encountered was like no other he could ever remember having.

He worked his tongue over the taut crest, then sucked a pearl into his mouth and explored the textures of both her and the pearl. He rolled the pearl over and around her nipple, tasting the flavors of both, savoring the intense heat of her and the serene coolness of the pearl.

"Damon."

His name had escaped her as a soft sound of delight, he thought with wonder, then felt her writhe beneath him. *Lord.* Making love to her disturbed him in a way he couldn't explain to himself, but he had no intention of stopping . . . even if he could. Beneath her openness his practiced, expert ways dissolved.

He pushed the pearls across her body, then back again. Alex cried out, taut and flushed by what was happening to her. The pearls were making hundreds of erotic rotations over her breasts, stomach, and thighs, bringing her skin to vibrant, pulsing life. It was a madness that sent curling, heavy heat to between her legs. Her hands clenched and unclenched on the satin sheets; her head tossed fretfully on the pillow; her hips undulated.

The strain of holding back was telling on Damon. A feverish urge had overtaken him. He was no longer sure what he was doing, only sure of what he must do. He needed to take her. Fill her. Saturate himself completely with the feeling of her so that he would never want her this way again.

She lifted one knee, drawing his gaze, and he saw the pearls slip between her legs. Gently he retrieved them, pulling them upward.

Alex felt each individual pearl as they passed against her. Nerves caught fire, and pleasure gripped her with an intense ecstasy that built and built. Would it stop, she wondered. And would she be whole when it ended? She hoped not.

He cupped a breast and guided a nipple into his mouth, and his fingers replaced the pearls between her legs. Raw, fiery sensations concentrated in Alex where he stroked, teasing, tormenting. Soundlessly her lips parted as her back arched off the bed.

Twilight in daylight.

Sounds of rapture, filling a room without sound.

Satin, pearls, and burning flesh.

With eyes glazed with desire she looked at him. "Make it now."

"I may have to hurt you," he said thickly.

She threaded her fingers into the black silkiness of his hair. "I'll come apart if you don't fill me soon."

"Dear Lord." He closed his eyes as a powerful wave of desire crashed over him, tearing away the last vestiges of his control. He positioned himself over her, quickly prepared himself, and sank deeply into her.

And at that moment he knew she was the most exciting woman he'd ever have.

Damon crossed his arms over his bare chest and waited grimly for what Graham was going to say.

"The shipment never made it to Nicaragua," Graham said. "Once again the attack was well-planned, well-executed. Again we lost six men and the entire arms shipment."

Damon erupted with a fierce expletive and slammed his fist against the teak paneling.

Graham waited until his employer subsided. "What are we going to do?"

"We suspend all shipments immediately."

Graham's blond eyebrows shot straight up. "*What?* We can't do that. We've got orders filled and waiting to go. People are depending on us. Deals have been made."

"Those deals aren't worth the paper they're written on if we can't deliver."

"Do you still think this is the work of Kito Sobota?"

"I know so. Have you started the surveillance on him I asked for yesterday?"

"You didn't ask for something easy, you know. This is one of the most wanted men in the world. What makes you think my men and I can find him when law enforcement agencies everywhere have failed?"

Damon eyed him steadily. "Because this is important."

Damon made his way slowly back to his stateroom and to Alex. But instead of returning to bed with her, he switched on a light across the room and chose a chair. Tired and worried, he rested his head against the chair's cushioned back.

What now? he thought. *What now?*

Alex stretched and opened her eyes. "Hi. Where have you been?"

"I had something to check on. I'm sorry I woke you."

She smiled dreamily. "I'm not." She rose and walked to Damon.

In the pale light, naked, with the rope of pearls around her neck and her hair wild, Alex looked to him like a goddess of desire. Damon hadn't expected to want her again tonight, and he was completely taken off guard by his hungry reaction as he watched her come to him. The pearls circled the outside of her breasts, framing them as a tantalizingly erotic picture.

As she nestled onto his lap, her scent gently embraced him—a scent of lovemaking and woman.

She wrapped an arm around his neck and leaned against him. "Make love to me," she whispered.

Damon felt as if something inside him exploded. He tangled his hand in her hair, holding her to him as he plundered her mouth with his tongue and his lips. His need for her approached violence, and it didn't make sense. But there was no time to reason out the matter. Not with her so hot and willing in his arms.

He lifted her and positioned her legs on either side of him. He bent his head and captured one stiffened nipple in his mouth. His whole body vibrated with urgency, making it impossible for him to be gentle.

Desire was his ruler. Her body was his goal.

He nibbled and sucked at her until Alex thought she would peak just from his mouth at her breast. A rapturous fever held her in its grip, and the heat was the strongest between her legs. Sitting on his lap with her legs straddling him, she was spread open to his hard, pulsing arousal with only the material of his trousers separating them. His desire pressed upward into her, touching sensitive, vulnerable points. She threaded her fingers through his hair, forcing a tighter suction on her nipple. He obliged. Moaning softly, she began rocking against him, straining for more contact, reaching blindly for the ultimate consummation. "Damon," she cried helplessly.

"Raise up," he ordered, a rough thickness in his voice.

He unzipped his pants. Then, both of them ready, he brought her down on him.

A soft scream escaped Alex, and she threw back her head as intense pleasure scored through and took her to ecstasy once, twice, three times. But Damon wasn't satisfied. There was something else he wanted from her. Something he had to have. And so he continued, rotating her hips over him, touching and kissing her in every place he could reach. Each time she peaked, he felt her inner contractions and became excited all over again. It will never end, he thought. And then it did, taking him unawares with its power.

Quivering and damp-skinned, Alex slumped against him. For several minutes they clung to each other. Then, still inside her, he stood and carried her to the bed.

His body throbbed with wanting her, he thought angrily, and he had just made love to her yet again. *What is wrong with me?* He rolled over to her and smoothed her hair away from her face, then stilled. "Where are your pearls, Alex?"

Her hand went to her bare neck. "I don't know. I had them on. . . ." She sat up, searching the area around her. Then she spotted them at the bottom of the bed, a long, luminous rope, coiled and gleaming on the oyster-hued satin. "Oh, no!"

Damon reached for them. "The string has been broken. I'm sorry. I guess I got carried away. My lovemaking must have been too rough."

Her distress melted away. "I can't imagine you being too rough."

His stomach began to flutter with fresh hot need. "I'll get them restrung for you. They probably need it anyway after being hidden away for so many years." He laid the pearls on the bedside table, turned back, and brought her firm, warm, softly curved body against his. "I know a jeweler in Paris who will do an excellent job. Tomorrow, two of my best men will take them."

Just for a moment she felt a stirring of uneasiness. But when his hand slipped between her legs and his mouth covered hers, she forgot it.

Five

Something surfaced from beneath the sea, closed a hand around Alex's ankle, and pulled her down into the blue Mediterranean. Then lips found hers and she tasted salt water, passion, and Damon. It was a taste worth drowning for, she thought hazily, wrapping her legs and arms tightly around his hard, lean form as the silky waters closed around them, enfolding them in its rapturous depths.

There was no air, no sound, no light. Only Damon.

And then there were all four.

They broke the surface, laughing and gasping for breath. She clung to him while he supported them treading water.

"Damon, we nearly drowned!"

"I couldn't resist. You looked like some exotic piece of flotsam."

"Excuse me? I looked like floating wreckage?"

He grinned. "Maybe I should have said mermaid."

"Sure. An auburn-haired mermaid wearing a gold bikini."

"I did say exotic."

"How long can you tread water?"

"Indefinitely."

She smiled, satisfied. "Good, because I'm very happy here. Wherever we are," she added as an afterthought.

"We're in a bay off the coast of Spain."

"Isn't that nice? Did you know that your skin feels like wet satin?" She wrapped herself tighter around him, and felt the muscles of his powerful body contract and expand as he worked to keep them afloat.

He groaned, half teasing, half serious. "Don't start anything, Alex, unless you'd like to find out what it's like to make love on the floor of the sea."

She grinned. "I'll make love with you anytime and anywhere you want."

He shook his head slowly. "You're a very dangerous lady."

"Funny, I've often thought how dangerous you are. Thank you for having the *Ares* stop here this morning."

He smiled, amused indulgence softening the hard lines of his face. A hundred yards behind her, he saw the *Ares* looming like a behemoth. "What else was I supposed to do? You said you'd rather swim in the sea than in the ship's pool."

"You seriously think I would choose a swimming pool over the Mediterranean?"

He chuckled. "No, I guess not. But what I *do* think is that you've been out in the sun long enough."

Her nose wrinkled with teasing disdain. "You're just getting tired."

"I'm concerned about you getting too much sun."

"You mean you wouldn't want me if I were all red and burned?"

"I'd want you if you looked like a lobster and had some foul-smelling unguent smeared all over you." He raised one black brow. "Do you want to test me?"

Giving up, she sighed, bent her head, and brushed a kiss along his jaw. "I suppose you're right, but it's so peaceful here."

"I tell you what. Let's go back. We'll shower and change, and then I'll have Benes serve your lunch on the afterdeck."

"*My* lunch? Where are you going to eat?"

"In my study." She groaned lightheartedly. "Hey" —briefly he caught her face in his large hands—"by the time you're finished, I'll be through with business for a while, and we'll spend some more time together."

"Okay, okay," she murmured.

"Race you back?"

"You'll lose," she said.

Her laughter was infectious. "What makes you think so?" he asked, smiling.

"Because I'm going to get a head start!" She broke free of him, lifted her arms, and ducked him, then struck out swimming.

"I was just about to give the captain a call to see why we haven't gotten under way yet," Damon said as Graham strode into his office. "Do you know anything about it?"

"Yeah. We've got a problem. Five minutes ago we received an anonymous tip that there's a bomb somewhere aboard this ship."

"Damn!" Damon stood and hurled his pen onto the desk. "Have you started a search?"

Graham nodded. "And divers are in the water."

"Good. Get all unnecessary personnel off—no, wait— Let me get Alex ashore first. I don't want her to know anything about this."

"All right." Graham jerked up the phone and punched two buttons. "Load Mr. Barand's car onto the launch immediately and get it ashore." When he hung up, he turned to Damon, who was impassively gathering papers and shoving them into a briefcase. "I just don't understand it. We have the best security available. How could this happen?"

"It's not so hard to figure out. Every time we stop, we're a sitting duck. It wouldn't take much— several chunks of plastic explosives on the hull, a couple of timers. Damn, we should have taken precautions on that score before now."

"I'm sorry—"

Damon held up his hand. "It's as much my fault as yours." He clicked shut the lock on the briefcase and straightened. "No one is to take any unnecessary chances, understand?"

"We should hit paved road soon," Damon said, guiding his big Mercedes over the rough lane that led up from the beach. Resting his elbow on the open window, he threw frequent glances into the rearview mirror until he could no longer see the *Ares*. "According to the map, there are several villages, the first one about twenty-five miles inland from here. They might be interesting to explore, and at any rate, we'll have a nice drive through the hills." She propped her back against the door and eyed him thoughtfully. Brushed cotton gabardine trousers stretched tautly across his thighs and the ice-blue linen sport shirt he wore was open at the throat. "I'm glad you had a change of heart about working this afternoon. But somehow you don't seem the type who would enjoy a simple drive through the hills. Are you doing this just for me?"

He cast a brief glance at her. She was wearing a summer frock made of a light and airy pale yellow material that lifted from her legs with every current of breeze. The bodice was cut low and fastened across her breasts by a line of small buttons. He had a sudden urge to stop the car, pull her into his arms, and absorb the flavors of her mouth into his with a hard kiss. He forced himself to be satisfied with bringing the back of her hand to his mouth for a light brush of his lips. "Of course I'm doing it for you. But I also plan to enjoy the afternoon. When I was a boy growing up in Prague, everything, even the air, seemed to be gray. The color and open feeling of the countryside appeals to me a great deal, especially this time of year."

That was probably the first bit of personal information he had given her—other than the fact that he and Kito had grown up together—and she wondered if he realized it. "I guess what I really meant was that you're such a driven man. You do nothing idly. I think when we were swimming this morning was the first time I'd seen you even close to being relaxed."

The easy fashion in which she could almost reach inside him and touch vital chords made him uncomfortable. Despite the fact that Kito was now a menacing presence in his life, he had been relaxed this morning, swimming with her in the peaceful waters of the bay. She had a way of making simple things enjoyable.

But at what cost had he relaxed, he mused. Now that same bay might end up to be the *Ares*'s graveyard.

"There are some things I do in a leisurely way," he drawled provocatively. "What about when I make love to you?"

"Then you're at your most intense," she said, her voice soft as if she were remembering his lovemaking.

Damn. He had meant to distract her, and she had ended up distracting him. He took a tighter grip on the steering wheel and stared straight ahead. "It's a warm day. We should be able to find a nice bottle of sparkling wine in one of these villages ahead, and no doubt some excellent paella."

"Turn there."

His foot came off the accelerator. "What?"

She pointed at the windshield. "Turn there. To the left. Let's see where that little road leads."

"Why?"

Her eyes sparkled with warm golden lights. "Why not?"

He turned the wheel to the left, leaving the lane for what was little more than a wide path. But the Mercedes took the furrows and grooves easily and soon they were in the middle of a field of bluebells and meadow saffrons.

"Oh, Damon, isn't it beautiful? Let's get out and walk."

This time he did as she asked without question. His face stern, his body tense, he got out of the car and came around to help her.

Alex set out across the meadow, very aware of Damon at her side. Since he had come out onto the afterdeck and insisted that he was in the mood to go ashore, Alex had sensed that something was troubling him. But she had learned enough about him to know that she wouldn't find out what was wrong until he was ready to tell her.

Even through the soft haze of her love for him, she could see certain things clearly about Damon.

He had an inclination to distrust immediately, and it required a conscious decision for him to let anyone close. In most people this inclination would be a weakness, and to a certain extent it was in him too. But given his line of work, it was also his strength. It seemed she had no other choice. She had to accept his ways.

With time, his love would come, and with his love, other changes. And in the meantime, she thought, she was with him. Fluffy white clouds reflected the soft glare of the afternoon sun down onto them. Bluebells in colors from pale china-blue to deep indigo swayed on their slender stems. Dotted among the bell-shaped flowers were white and red sea lavender, and cream and burgundy hollyhock.

She and Damon walked through the sea of flowers until they came upon a brook with water so clear they could see the stones that lay on its bottom. Thrift grew on the banks, forming a downy cushion of pale to dark pink flowers. Sweet-scented umbrella pines and lemon trees, whose boughs held juicy, fat fruit, spread their roots along the water's edge.

Tense and on edge, Damon shielded his eyes and gazed up at the sun. "Maybe we should go back to the car."

"Not just yet. It's cool and shady here. Let's stay awhile." She bent and dipped her hands into the brook. "The water is great," she said, and promptly kicked off her sandals and waded in.

"Alex—"

The water struck her at mid-calf. She held out her hand to him. "Come on in. It's wonderful."

He shoved his hands in the pockets of his trousers and shook his head. She shrugged and took a few steps against the current.

"Alex, dammit, be careful. You're going to cut your feet on those rocks."

She bent, scooped up a handful of the pebbles and stones, and studied them. "Some of them have the loveliest colors in them, and they're not rough or sharp-edged at all. Think of how many years these waters have rolled these stones to smoothness."

He watched her, annoyed. She looked so beautiful, her head bent over those stupid stones as if she were holding a handful of jewels. But, he reminded himself, she wasn't beautiful.

Still . . . the sun slipped through the branches and leaves of the trees and fell over her head like a fine golden rain, making the long strands of her hair glisten with a rich redness. And the sun gave her skin a pearlescent luster. But he had thought that before and he had been wrong then too.

Gently she tossed the rocks back into the brook, then bent again, this time to splash water onto her bare legs. The front of her dress gaped open, giving him an enticing view of her breasts.

"Ah, this is nice. So cool." She palmed wetness over her slender arms and up to her throat. Then she straightened, and crystal droplets of water slid down her neck and into the bodice of her dress.

Damn. He was becoming aroused just watching her.

She stooped and with two hands brought up water to her mouth. "It's wonderful. You have to have a drink."

He swallowed hard. The water that didn't make her mouth slipped down her throat to the front of her dress, wetting it. "I don't want a drink."

"But I've never had more delicious water. Aren't you thirsty?" She offered him the cool, sweet water in her cupped hands. "Come on," she said with tempting beguilement. "Just take a sip."

His eyes were on her breasts where her stiff nipples pushed enticingly against the damp material. "A sip?"

Her laughter was like the ring of a crystal bell. "Damon, the water's seeping out of my hands. Hurry."

Slowly he walked toward her, through the bluebells and crocuses and the cushiony pink thrift that blanketed the water's edge, and into the brook, unmindful of his custom-made Italian leather shoes. When he stopped in front of her, she grinned ruefully. "You're too late. See?" She held up her empty hands, then cupped her wet palms against his cheeks. "But it feels good, doesn't it?"

"I know something else that would feel good," he muttered thickly.

Her smile faded and her pulse quickened as she saw the desire burning in his eyes. "What?"

"I'll show you." He swept her into his arms, carried her to the bank, and lay her down in the fragrant grass. Then he was on top of her. "You said you'd make love to me anytime, anywhere. Did you mean it?"

Her arms curled around his neck. "Try me."

He groaned as a wave of heat engulfed him. "Alex, why can't I get enough of you?" He didn't give her a chance to answer, but attacked her mouth with his, kissing her harder than he'd ever kissed her before.

He reached between them, hastily unbuttoned the front of her sundress, and pushed the fabric aside. Then he tore his mouth from her lips, fastened onto a breast and sucked while he massaged the other breast.

Alex fumbled at the waistband of his trousers, responding to his urgency.

At her touch he involuntarily contracted his stomach muscles, allowing her hand access to the inside of his trousers. But as soon as she touched him, he realized he was too far gone with need to withstand her caressing strokes. Half mad, he shoved her skirt around her waist and then grappled for her panties. In his frenzy he tore them from her body.

The azure, bell-shaped flowers drooped from their stems and swayed with the gentle breeze. Crickets chaffed somewhere nearby, and small insects hummed in the air. The velvety down of the hollyhock broadcast its sweet scent and lured a bee to inspect the deep interior of its blossom.

A frantic need was upon him. As soon as he freed himself from his trousers, he entered her.

And there in the lovely, wild meadow, beneath the Spanish sun, he took her.

"We didn't find any sign of a bomb," Graham said.

Damon stood on the bridge and gazed at the rapidly receding Spanish shoreline. "That's good. From now on, when we're at anchor, arrange for a team of divers to patrol."

"Right," Graham said, then plowed his fingers through his hair. "Why, Damon? I mean, why at this particular time is all this happening? The hijackings. The bomb scare."

A muscle worked in Damon's jaw. "There's only one person who can tell us that, and he's not talking yet. Have you learned anything from your surveillance of him?"

"Surveillance, *hell*." Graham shook his head, amazed and disgusted. "Kito's as slippery as a damned eel. First I think we've got him located for sure. Then he's reported on another continent." He hesitated. "I want to make sure I understand you perfectly on this. *All* you want us to do is try to keep Kito under surveillance and to find out what he's up to in regards to you—is that right?"

"That's right," Damon said firmly. "You're not to lay a finger on him."

His body sheened with sweat, Damon rolled off Alex, flung his arm over his forehead, and stared at the ceiling.

Each time he had her, he told himself it would be the last. And then he would take her again. And then again.

A hard breath shuddered through him. *Damn.* He was even trembling.

This fascination he had for her had to stop now.

The memory of his unplanned, frenzied taking of her in the flowered meadow still remained with him, like a perfectly focused, vividly colored photograph. In the days following that afternoon, his passion for her had been held in check only by the slender threads of his determination. But those threads were growing increasingly weak.

Even now, after his body should have been sated with her, it took every ounce of will he had not to reenter her . . . and stay there forever.

He wasn't used to acting or feeling like this. No part of him remained unaffected by their lovemaking. His need for Alex had grown to near obsession.

If he added his troubles with Kito to his preoccupation with Alex, the control of his world seemed to be slipping out of his hands. It scared him, and that he couldn't have.

He felt her hand tangle in his chest hair, then come to rest over his heart.

"Your vacation should be just about over, shouldn't it?" he asked casually.

Completely caught off guard by the question, Alex stiffened.

"When is your company expecting you back to work?"

"The original plan was for me to return two days from now. But I—"

He sat up and reached for his robe. "I'll make immediate arrangements for you to be flown back."

"Damon—"

"This way, you'll have time to get over your jet lag before you have to go back to work."

Alex felt as if she had been unexpectedly and brutally attacked by an enemy she didn't know.

"I'll send Benes to your room to help you pack," Damon said, dropped a kiss on her cheek, and started for the door.

Say something, she ordered herself. *Make him stop and come back so that you can talk and find out what's happened.* "Damon?"

He stopped but didn't turn around. "Yes?"

"What about my pearls?" was all she could think to say.

"I'll have them sent to you as soon as they're restrung. Good-bye."

Stunned and incapable of moving, Alex lay on the oyster-satin sheets that still carried the evocative scent of their lovemaking. Within the space of sixty seconds her hopes and dreams had been destroyed.

She had wanted to tell him of her plans to call her manager and inform him that she would be extending her vacation. But now she realized that Damon had known of her intentions. He wanted her to leave.

Feeling as if all life had left her, she slowly crawled out of bed and made her way to her stateroom. With Benes's assistance, she was packed and ready to leave the ship within the hour.

Damon stood on the bridge deck and watched as the helicopter carrying Alex lifted off from the *Ares*, circled, then headed away, its destination Barcelona's Prat de Llobregat Airport, where a charter jet waited.

It was best this way, he thought, holding his hands behind his back in a fierce grip.

In the helicopter Alex gave a final wave at the solitary figure on the bridge. He did not wave back.

Craning her neck, she kept Damon in sight for as long as she could. She waited, and when the *Ares* was nothing but a dot on the horizon, she let the tears begin to fall.

Six

Alex slumped farther down in the doctor's office chair. "I know I suggested you do a pregnancy test, but I was really hoping I just had the flu. It's running rampant at my company."

"You're pregnant," the doctor repeated.

She dropped her head in her hands, still in shock from the news. "I've stayed so busy lately." *Deliberately.* "And then the flu swept through the company and increased my workload."

"You do seem a little run-down. We've done the blood workup and I should have the rest of the results in about a week. In the meantime, I suggest you quit pushing yourself so hard and get plenty of rest. I'll prescribe prenatal vitamins, but on the whole you're in good health. There should be no problem." He picked up his pen and began scratching notes on her chart.

Minutes later Alex sat in her car in the parking lot outside the doctor's office, staring blindly through the windshield. *She was going to have a baby.* The idea terrified her. The idea thrilled her.

Weeks had passed since her return to Connecticut, and her heartache had not abated. But she had determinedly picked up the threads of her life and continued. She had not shirked her responsibilities at work or turned down one social invitation. And if she had lost weight and begun to look drawn, her friends had had the good sense not to comment on it, at least not in her presence.

She had given everything she had to Damon, and it hadn't been enough to win his love. So be it, she thought. She could not stop loving him, but she also could not let it affect the rest of her life.

Damon's baby. For the first time since confirming her suspicions of pregnancy, she placed her hand on her stomach, and a sweet, serene happiness flooded over her. At that moment her future clearly stretched before her. As Charlotte had raised her, so, too, would she raise this child—alone and with all the love she had and all the wisdom she could summon up.

Only one doubt remained. Should she tell Damon? She had no illusions that the knowledge of the baby would miraculously change Damon's feeling toward her. Or that he would want his son or daughter. He had been too strict about using precautions when they made love. In fact, this baby wouldn't even be growing inside her if it hadn't been for a sunny day and a Spanish meadow.

But did he have a right to know?

"I've thought of nothing else for the last twenty-four hours, Zan," she said into the phone. "And I've come to the decision that Damon has a right to know about his child. That's why I need you to find out for me where he is."

"You're not thinking straight, and it's no wonder. You're feeling sick as a dog, you said so yourself. Let me send one of our planes for you. Come to me. Let me take care of you."

She smiled to herself. Inbred into Zan's genes was the imperious attitude that there was nothing beyond the scope of his power, even the ability to make better an unwed friend's pregnancy. "I love you for being concerned, Zan, but I can take care of myself." She heard him give a most unroyal snort, and quickly added, "Don't say what you're thinking. I have no regrets about the time I had with Damon."

"All right. But I will say that I don't think Damon Barand has any rights at all, and I think it would be a grave mistake to contact him."

"Wouldn't you want to know if you had a child somewhere in the world?"

"Of course. But that's different."

"Why?"

"Because . . . well, just because."

"Zan, do this for me. Find out where he is and what I have to do to get in touch with him."

"Dammit, Alex."

"Zan, I just want to go to him, tell him, then come back home and get on with my life. Argue with me when I'm stronger, okay?"

"Oh, all right. I'll get back to you with the information. But promise me that if you need anything at all, you'll call me. If that bastard hurts you again, I'll raise up our whole damned army against him."

Alex remembered her conversation with Zan as less than twenty-four hours later the helicopter in which she rode circled above the *Ares* and prepared to land. He had called her back with the information that the *Ares* was in the Aegean, cruising the Greek islands, and he had given her instructions on how to place a call to the ship.

She had not been able to get through to Damon. For all his good-natured ways, Graham was exceedingly effective in shielding Damon from people to whom he had no wish to speak. Determined, she had told Graham it was imperative that she see Damon as soon as possible. Within the hour Graham had called back to arrange her visit.

The helicopter landed with precision on the ship's pad, and Graham was there to open the door for her even before the rotors stopped turning.

"It's nice to see you again, Alex," he said, giving her a helping hand down. He scanned her face and frowned. "I hope the flight didn't make you airsick?"

Alex grinned wryly. Wanting to be as comfortable as possible on the trip, she had worn pale green slacks with a matching blouse that was cool and loose, and a quick look in the mirror before she had left the Athens airport had told her that her skin and the green of her outfit were close to the same shade. However, the condition wasn't due to the jet that had carried her from Connecticut to Athens or the helicopter that had brought her to the *Ares*. "We did have a little turbulence, but all in all the trip was fine."

"Good." He gestured with his hand. "Come this way. Damon is waiting."

She started off, but had a thought and stopped. "Could you please have the helicopter wait for me? I don't expect our visit will take long."

Graham's expression remained perfectly bland. "Of course." Minutes later he ushered her into Damon's office and quietly shut the door behind her.

Alex faced Damon across the wide expanse of carpet.

Since her call Damon had dreaded this moment. And waited impatiently for this moment. During the time that had passed since he'd last seen her, he had awakened more nights than he cared to admit, his body aching for her and drenched in sweat, and in his effort to forget her, he had tried other women. But each time, his interest in the woman of the moment had waned and he had sent her on her way before he had even taken her to bed.

He had fiercely resisted the idea of Alex coming here. He wanted above all else to get her out of his bloodstream.

But he hadn't been able to stop himself from saying yes.

He rose and gestured toward a chair. "Won't you sit down?"

"Thank you." Such politeness from two people who had been lovers, she thought with odd detachment as she crossed the room and took a seat.

He settled back into his big Cordovan leather chair and with one all-encompassing glance took in everything about her. God, why was she so pale? He had promised himself that he would let her speak first, but the words slipped out before he could stop them. "You look tired, Alex. Couldn't you rest on the flight?"

The barest of smiles touched her lips. "I haven't been well lately."

A pain tied knots in his stomach. "I'm sorry to hear that."

The formality of his words didn't affect her as they once might have, she realized thankfully. Her bone-hurting weariness gave her the advantage of total indifference to the outcome of this talk. She was here only because she sincerely believed she was doing the right thing. "Damon, I don't want to take any more of your time than necessary, so I'll get straight to the point. I'm pregnant, and I thought you should know."

He did not so much as flinch. From her seat in front of his desk she could not even discern a blink. He also did not say anything.

She sighed and briefly rubbed her forehead. She had made reservations at the Caravel in Athens, and the heavenly prospect of the waiting bed made her next words clipped and brisk.

"I'll save you the bother of asking the usual questions," she said. "Yes, the baby is yours. No, I'm not here to demand marriage or anything else from you. I simply felt you had the right to know. Now that you do, I'll go." She stood up.

"Sit down." His voice was as hard as steel, and his black gaze was sharp enough to cut a diamond. He waited until she sank back into the chair, then said, "Now, start over again."

She shrugged, wondering why he was so angry and noticing that her forehead was beaded with perspiration. "I'm pregnant."

"When did you find out?"

"Two days ago. I went to the doctor, hoping I just had the flu."

"The doctor took the appropriate tests?"

"Yes." She licked her bottom lip with her tongue. "Do you think I might have something to drink? Perhaps some ginger ale?"

Without taking his eyes from her, he lifted the receiver of his phone from its cradle and punched a button. "Bring Miss Sheldon an iced ginger ale immediately." Hanging up, he asked, "Would you like to lie down for a while?"

Yes, she thought, and reached into her purse for a handkerchief to pat the perspiration on her face. "No, thank you. As soon as I have some of the ginger ale, I'll be on my way."

"You're not going anywhere."

"But I have reservations—"

"You're not going anywhere," he repeated. "Did you really think you could come here, tell me you were carrying my baby, and then leave?"

She looked at him oddly. "Yes."

Benes entered the room, and with a friendly smile came to her side and handed her a tall, cold crystal glass of ginger ale. "It is so nice that you are back with us, Miss Sheldon."

"Thank you, Benes, but I'm here just for a short visit."

A curt wave from Damon wiped the smile from Benes's face and sent him hurrying out of the room.

"Why are you so ill, Alex?" he asked softly.

She took a sip of the drink and smiled without humor. "I'm not ill; I'm pregnant."

"Is that all? There's nothing more?"

She shook her head. "I'll be fine soon, or, worse-case scenario, I'll be fine in about seven and a half months. I understand some women feel ill the whole term of their pregnancy. But that's no concern of yours." She took another sip of the ginger ale, then set the glass on his desk. "If you like, I'll let you know when the baby is born and whether it's a boy or a girl."

"Then you're not planning an abortion?"

"No." Why didn't he understand what she was saying? "Damon, I'm going to have this baby. But don't worry, I expect this to be the last time I contact you in person. And if you don't want to know—"

"Why do you expect this to be the last time you contact me?"

He was *really* furious, and she was beginning to regret the effort she had made to come to tell him about the baby. "Damon, I'm trying very hard to make my intentions clear. Just listen to what I'm saying. I'm not going to bother you again. I'll even sign a legal document to that effect if you like."

"That's very considerate of you." He jerked up the phone and jabbed another button. "Get Miss Sheldon's luggage from the helicopter and place it in the stateroom she had before." He hung up the phone, stood, came around the desk, and reached down for her, bringing her to her feet. "Come on, Alex. You're going to bed before you pass out on me."

She swayed, and his hands caught and steadied her. Feeling that she had to try one more time to get through to him, she said, "There's no need for you to feel responsible for me, Damon. I know you don't want a child, and I don't blame you in any way. You always took such care with precautions. It was just that once. At any rate, *I* want this baby, and I can provide for it and—"

He placed a finger over her mouth. "When you've had some rest, we'll talk."

Oh, hell, she thought wearily. The trip and this meeting had taken a tremendous toll on her. At this point she wasn't even sure she could make it to the Caravel. She'd stay here tonight, she decided, and then start her trip back tomorrow.

He led her to the sunrise-colored stateroom, and as soon as he had made sure she had everything she needed, he left her. Too tired and nauseated to object, she took a quick shower and donned her long, cool, cotton nightgown, climbed into bed, and slipped into a deep sleep.

Damon couldn't take his eyes off Alex. She was lying on her back, one hand curled beside her face, the other across her stomach, sleeping so heavily, she almost seemed drugged.

He had had occasion to observe her asleep during the time she had spent with him. Even then she maintained that special light that fascinated him so. Now all her shining vibrancy was gone. Never had he seen her in such an exhausted slumber.

Had the baby forming inside her done this to her? Damn, he felt helpless. He wanted to help her, but he had no idea what to do for her.

He allowed himself a small smile. At least her honesty hadn't been affected, or her determination. She had made it perfectly clear that she planned on taking full responsibility for his child.

His child.

He shifted in his chair, straightened one leg, and reached into his trouser pocket for the delicate gold cross he constantly carried with him. Without looking at it, he held it.

Alex floated slowly and reluctantly free of the enshrouding cottony clouds that had protected her while she slept. Her eyelids lifted slightly, then closed against the light. She waited a few minutes, then tried opening her eyes again.

She blinked against the light from the small bedside lamp. Then she saw Damon. His chair was drawn close, and he was staring at her.

"How are you feeling?" he asked.

She swallowed against the dryness in her throat. "Less tired."

"Good. I'll have dinner served whenever you're ready."

She sat up and pushed a handful of hair out of her eyes. Earlier, when she had faced him in the study, she had been exhausted, benumbed by the trip, and concerned with what she had to tell him. The circumstances had given her a certain immunity against him. Now, though, the potency of his masculinity fairly jumped the small space between them, touching her, making her remember how much she loved him and making her yearn for things that could not be.

The time had obviously come for her to leave. "I'd like you to make arrangements for my trip back to Connecticut now."

"Alex," he said softly. "You're carrying my child. Do you really think I'd let you leave easily."

She was surprised by his question. "Of course I do."

"Then you don't know me at all."

"I never did."

"Then stay and get to know me."

She studied him for a minute and her eyes held a grave question. "Is that possible?"

Damon felt the imprint of the cross in his palm and realized that Alex had a point. There was a place in him he had never let anyone get past, and he wasn't sure he was capable of letting her be the first. "I want very much for you to stay, Alex."

The earnest appeal in his voice disturbed her. She slipped to the edge of the bed and stood. A brief spell of dizziness caused her to blindly reach out for something solid. It was Damon's hand she found, but his touch brought heat. As soon as the room stilled, she moved away from him.

At the mirror above the mother-of-pearl dressing table, she caught sight of herself. She ran a hand through her hair automatically, but quickly gave up trying to improve her appearance. It didn't matter. Her gaze dropped instead to the dressing table's iridescent surface and the Fabergé egg there. "What's this doing here?"

Just for a moment she had the impression he

was as puzzled as she. "I don't know," he finally said. "I guess I thought you might like to see it there when you woke up."

She regarded him in the mirror. "I can't stay here with you."

"Why not? If it's your business you're concerned about, it can be run by your manager. And if not, I'll get someone in there who can. You'll have our satellite hookup here, enabling you to keep in constant communication. Meetings can be arranged anytime you wish. We'll simply fly your people in."

She turned and leaned back against the dressing table. Memories of a time when this moment would have meant the world to her played through her mind. But there was a difference now. He wanted her to stay with him only because she was pregnant and not because of any feelings he might have for her. It had to be that.

"Tell me exactly what you have in mind, Damon."

He stood and shoved his hands into the pockets of his trousers. "I want to take care and provide for the baby. And you. I want us to be married."

His words went through her like a series of shock waves, leaving her weak. She crossed the room, climbed back into bed, and shut her eyes.

He gazed down at her, troubled. She looked so frail, so fragile. Defenseless. Her soft blue cotton gown with its lace-trimmed yoked bodice and deep ruffled hem reminded him of one a little girl might wear. He wasn't used to moderating his actions for others. His inclination was to make arrangements for a civil ceremony with all due haste. But his instincts told him she wouldn't be able to stand long enough for them to be married. He bent and laid his hand on her forehead. Did she feel warmer than normal?

"I want a doctor to look at you, Alex."

"I've been to a doctor," she mumbled. "Time will solve what's wrong with me."

Alex felt him sit down on the bed beside her and take her hand. Strangely she was comforted, and she remembered all the times in the past when he had reached for her hand.

She had never meant this visit to the *Ares* to last any longer than fifteen minutes, thirty minutes maximum. But now that she was there, she found she was reluctant to leave. And the reason wasn't all physical.

Right from the first, Damon had exerted a powerful force on her. Deep down inside her there had always been a crazy sense that she belonged with him; and, unfortunately, seeing him again was only reinforcing that belief. She had to forcibly remind herself of the pain she had suffered because of that belief.

"I want to take care of you and the baby. Please stay and let me." Emotion roughened and lowered his voice.

Her eyelids lifted and she stared into his black eyes. The intensity and depth there surprised her.

"Alex, I know you have every reason in the world to distrust me, and probably nothing I can say at this moment can change that. But, hopefully, time will prove to you I'm earnest in my desire to be a good husband and a good father."

"If I asked you why this was so important to you, would you tell me?"

"I would if I could. The problem is, I'm not sure I would be able to express coherently what I'm feeling. I haven't looked inside myself for a long time. Deliberately."

He had just told her a great deal. But . . . "I don't know, Damon. I just don't know."

"At least let us try," he whispered imploringly.

A tiny seed of hope moved and shifted inside her. Was it remotely possible that this baby she was carrying represented a new chance for her and Damon? She was unsure whether she could risk believing again; but then, she was unsure whether she could risk *not* believing. Whatever her doubts—and she did have them—there was no mistaking his sincerity.

"Alex?"

"All right, Damon. We can try."

It was the morning of his wedding.

Damon stood on the afterdeck of the *Ares* and gazed east toward the rising sun. He had never before considered marriage. The idea of uniting his life with another was an alien concept to him. The very word marriage implied an intimacy to which he had never before wanted to be involved.

His life up to now had been filled with the blood

and thunder of the wars he helped to perpetuate with his arms. Since the age of eight, inner peace had escaped him. But he had learned purpose. And he had come to understand death and violence. Most of all, he had come to understand control and power and the idea of protecting oneself.

But he had never been able to comprehend intimacy of the heart between two people.

Now he was about to take as his wife a woman who did not guard herself against him, who saw beauty where he did not, who could make him want her until he was near madness.

He had sent her away because his intense passion for her disturbed and confused him. He asked her to stay because her absence from his life had caused the very same turbulent emotions.

And because of the baby she carried.

The baby. The idea of a child frightened him, but not as much as it filled him with wonder.

He had been alone for such a long time, and now he was going to have a wife and a child.

"Good morning, Damon. Beautiful day for a wedding."

He shook away his thoughts and turned to Graham. "Good morning. How are things going?"

"Everything's on schedule, despite, or because of Soukapolis—I'm not sure which."

Damon smiled. Thaddeus Soukapolis, a friend and business associate of his, had put his private airstrip and docking facilities on the Greek island of his birth at Damon's disposal.

"Thaddeus is so excited about this wedding, you'd think it was his," Damon said.

"I understand he's had a few weddings of his own."

"A few."

"Well, at any rate, the guests should start arriving in about three hours at the Soukapolis airstrip."

Damon picked up a heavy silver coffeepot and poured himself a cup. "Anything on Kito?"

Graham shook his head unhappily. "He's got a group of intelligent, savvy men going around in circles. I'm sorry. We'll keep trying."

Damon stared back over the water, sipping the hot coffee. "He's been too quiet for the last few weeks. I don't like it."

"He and his men managed to get off with three of our arms shipments. Maybe he's satisfied."

"Not a chance."

Graham made a tentative gesture with his hand. "You know, maybe it might help me if I knew what was between you and Kito. I mean, I know you two grew up together, but—"

"It wouldn't help." Damon turned away.

Behind his back, Graham gave a silent whistle. The subject of Kito was an extremely sensitive one with Damon, and he couldn't help but be curious. He was also concerned. However, he recognized a brick wall when he saw one. "Would you like me to have your breakfast sent out here?"

Damon nodded.

"Okay. See you later."

Damon sipped his coffee and decided that perhaps the reason some wounds never healed was that they were so deep inside a person's soul, no air could reach the trauma. In his trouser pocket he found the cross and ran his fingers over the smooth gold.

Chessy. He could see her so clearly, laughing up at him, her long brown hair blowing in the wind, the cross glittering at her neck. So beautiful, so young.

"Where would you like your breakfast served, sir?"

Ice slid down Damon's spine.

"Perhaps this table, sir?"

Slowly Damon turned and faced Kito.

Kito's dark hair was layered long around his head, a beard covered his face, and he was dressed in an immaculately white waiter's uniform. He was harder than when Damon had last seen him, but the fanaticism in his eyes burned brighter . . . and the sadness.

"Happy wedding day, Damon."

"Where's Benes?"

"He was busy." Kito lifted the silver dome from a plate and inspected its contents. "The cook scrambled your eggs, I'm afraid. I tried to tell him that you liked your eggs poached, like Cilka used to do for you, remember? But the kitchen is in an uproar what with all the food they have to prepare today, and the chef just wasn't interested in listening to a temporary waiter hired only for the occasion."

Damon rested his hips against the railing and

folded his arms over his chest. Below him, on the quay, his security men patrolled. If he gave a signal, they'd come running. He didn't move.

"I've been waiting for you," he said.

"I know." For an instant a grin lit up Kito's face like the bright, brief flare of a flashbulb, then the light burned out. "Cilka's dead."

Pain made Damon briefly close his eyes. "When?"

"Two months ago." Kito poked absently at the linen napkin on the tray. "Mama died peacefully."

"I'm glad."

"I wasn't able to be there." His voice was without inflection. "The authorities had been keeping an eye on her in hopes of catching me. But the last time I was with her, she spoke of you." He picked up the silver spoon Damon had used to stir his coffee, and studied it. "She thought of you as her son."

"Cilka was a good woman. She raised me from the time I was eight years old, right along side you and Chessy."

"You know that when you left, you broke her heart . . . and Chessy's."

Damon expelled a heavy breath. "Cilka understood why I had to leave. She said so in a letter that caught up with me a year later."

The spoon clattered as it hit the glass surface of the table. "That was my mother. Always understanding and forgiving. She told you about Chessy in that letter, too, didn't she?"

"Yes."

He reached for the silver coffeepot and poured

himself a cup. "I hope you don't mind. I put an extra cup on the tray for me."

Damon nodded and waited. He knew that his abrupt departure had left things unfinished and unsaid between them.

"Cilka made me promise that I wouldn't seek revenge against you, but with her death, I am no longer held by that promise." He took a sip of the coffee.

Damon stroked a finger across his brow. "I wondered why now, after all these years."

"Now you know."

"You've hijacked enough of my arms to start your own war."

Kito's grin came quickly again. "And I'm not finished yet."

"Yes, you are. I've suspended all shipments indefinitely."

Kito sat the coffee cup down, stuck his hands in his pockets, and gazed at the horizon. "My cause is just, Damon. Because of it, I've done good works."

"Good!" Damon came away from the railing. "I've seen the headlines, Kito. How can you call senseless violence good?"

"You never understood."

"And that's why I left. You're a famous man, Kito. One of the most wanted men in the world. People say you're brilliant. I say you're over the edge."

Kito's head snapped around. "You're a sanctimonious bastard, Damon. Your arms sales have caused more deaths than I ever could."

"My weapons are used by trained soldiers in wars. I don't go into airports or cafés and indiscriminately gun down everyone I see, women and children included. I don't throw bombs into hotel lobbies, take hostage planeloads of holiday travelers, or assassinate politicians."

"No, but you do go off and leave a young girl pregnant, don't you? So that she has to suffer her shame alone. So that she feels driven to get a back-alley abortion and then when it goes bad she's too frightened and ashamed to come to her family for help and so she dies all alone, and her soul is condemned to eternal unrest."

Damon had known what was coming and met Kito's eyes without flinching. "Chessy didn't tell me she was pregnant. If I'd known I never would have left. As it was, I planned to bring her out as soon as I could. Believe that, Kito."

"I can't, damn you. *I can't!*" Unexpectedly the tension drained out of Kito's body. "Alex is a very nice lady," he said almost casually. "But I feel sorry for her. She doesn't know that you'll destroy her."

"This is between you and me, Kito. Leave Alex out of it."

Kito bent to the task of removing the dishes from the breakfast tray and arranging them on the table. When he was finished, he straightened and looked at Damon. "How do you exact revenge upon a man, Damon? That's a question I asked myself about you. You'll be glad to know that the question wasn't easily answered. You're not a man who can be bought, nor can you be broken. But I decided you could be irritated, so I stole the arms shipments and arranged for the bomb threat. I also decided you could be made to suffer." He smiled. "Your suffering will start shortly, Damon. Then I'll kill you."

"You'll try."

"Oh, I'll do it." Picking up the tray, he smiled. "Have a nice wedding, Damon. Carry Chessy's cross in your pocket. And when you're standing at the altar with Alex, see my sister's face and think of how beautiful she would have looked as a bride."

Kito left. And still, Damon didn't call for security.

Seven

The ivory satin wedding dress slipped over Alex's head and settled around her with shimmering elegance. Marie, Charlotte's longtime dressmaker, began fastening the long row of satin buttons at the back of the simple, classically styled dress.

Alex gazed with satisfaction at the image the cheval mirror cast back at her. She had arranged her auburn hair into a glossy pile on the top of her head; her brown eyes, no longer dull, shone with bright happiness; and her skin had its healthy glow back.

The nausea, aching weakness, and lassitude had gradually disappeared, until today, less than an hour away from her wedding, she felt in good health and guardedly optimistic about the future.

"You made the right choice," Marie said, "not

wearing a veil. The coronet of orange blossoms will be exactly the right touch."

Alex glanced at the seamstress she had asked Damon to fly over from Connecticut. "I can't thank you enough for the dress. Believe me, I know how hard you and your workers have labored to get it ready."

Marie smiled and turned to the task of pulling and tugging the many folds of the long skirt into place. "It was my pleasure and a chance of a life-time. How often does someone like me get to work on a dress like this? And for such a glamorous event?"

"Glamorous?" Finding it hard to stand still, Alex eased away from Marie's fussy attentions and crossed to the bed. Leaning down, she fingered the ivory satin ribbon that twined among the creamy orange blossoms of her coronet.

"*And* exclusive. Think about it. This is a mar-riage between a billionaire and a millionaire, tak-ing place aboard the world's largest private yacht, at the dock of a famous Greek shipping tycoon. The paparazzi will be out in force, and photos of the dress I made will be seen around the world."

A frown marred Alex's smooth forehead. "Damon has assured me the press will be kept well away from the ship. I don't want this turned into a circus."

"Haven't you ever heard of telephoto lenses?"

A knock on the door forestalled Alex's response. Marie went to the door and opened it. "Oh, no! You can't come in here, Mr. Barand."

Alex swiveled and took in his expression. "Damon, has something happened? You look so serious."

He hadn't realized she would be able to pick up on his mood with such ease. Deliberately he lightened his mood. "Isn't that how a man is supposed to look on his wedding day?"

She regarded him thoughtfully. There were so many deep and mysterious currents and eddies in his life. Would she ever be able to find a place in it? "I suppose so."

The dressmaker's face reflected horror as she followed Damon into the room. "Mr. Barand, you really should leave. The groom can't see the bride before the wedding."

"Don't worry, Marie. Rules have never applied to Alex and me." He smiled at Alex. "Isn't that right?"

Alex's heart beat faster now that Damon was in the room. He hadn't finished dressing yet, and wore only the oxford-gray striped pants and the white winged-collar shirt of his wedding attire. There were gray pearl studs part of the way up his shirt, but the collar had been left open, exposing the bronze column of his throat.

"Yes," she said.

"Marie, will you please excuse us?"

He waited until the seamstress had gone, then he crossed to Alex. "How are you feeling?"

"I don't know if it's the extraordinary clarity of the air here in the Greek islands or the care everyone on board has been giving me, but I'm back to my old self."

"You look beautiful," he said, and then realized with a jolt of amazement that it was true. No matter how often in the past he had told himself differently, Alex *was* beautiful. "I brought you something."

For the first time, she noticed that he was carrying a large square black velvet jeweler's box. "My pearls?" she asked with mixed feelings. Damon's fixation with them had insured she could no longer think of the pearls with the same enjoyment and warmth she once had.

He opened the box and held it out to her. "I hounded the jeweler to make sure they would be back in time for the wedding."

She lifted the heavy, gleaming pearl rope from the box. There had been times in the past weeks when she had wondered if she would ever see them again, and there had been times when she had hoped she never would.

"Will you wear the necklace today?" he asked.

She hesitated. "The neckline of this dress really doesn't need them."

"I'll leave the decision up to you," he said evenly, and held out another jeweler's box, this one smaller, and snapped open the lid. Earrings designed in a heart shape that matched the shape of the necklace's clasp, and rendered in sparkling diamonds and small, perfect pearls nestled against the black velvet.

"It would have been impossible to find pearls that matched those of your necklace, so I decided to go for the feeling, something that wouldn't detract from the necklace but would be a subtle accent. Do you like them?"

"They're lovely," she murmured, "and it means a lot to me that you had them made for me."

He raised her face and gazed solemnly down at her. "I want you to know that I'm going to do everything in my power to make sure you're happy." He placed a gentle kiss on her cheek. "I'll see you in about thirty minutes."

"Watch this, Alex," Thaddeus Soukapolis called. He stripped out of his white suitcoat, placed a fully set, small wooden table between his teeth, and proceeded to dance across the bare floor of the outdoor terrace of the taverna to the music of bouzoukis.

Thaddeus, an exuberant silver-haired barrel-chested man who ran his shipping line and private life with equal zest and energy, had insisted that the wedding reception be moved from the *Ares* to his favorite beachside taverna. But the taverna hadn't been able to hold the ever-growing numbers of villagers who mingled happily with the elegant wedding guests, and the reception had spilled out into the yard. The afternoon was awash with laughter and music; the air was scented with the blossoms of lemons and kumquats. Two goats grazed contentedly nearby.

The gaiety that surrounded them was infectious, and Alex laughed up at Damon. "Look at Thaddeus. Isn't he incredible? Oh, I'm so glad we came here."

His arm tightened around her waist. "Then I'm glad too."

The table crashed to the flagstone terrace. Thaddeus charged across the open space and embraced Alex in an enthusiastic bear hug. "How is the beautiful bride? Are you having a good time?"

She was nearly breathless when she managed to extricate herself from his arms. "Yes, and it was wonderful of you to arrange all of this for us."

Thaddeus clapped his hand on Damon's shoulder. "For my friend, nothing is too good." He turned to Zan, who had been standing quietly beside Alex. "And Prince Al Iraj, it is an honor to have you here in the village of my birth."

"I am honored to be here," Zan said, his gaze sliding toward Alex, telling her without words that whether he approved or not, he would be damned if he'd miss her wedding.

With a private smile reserved just for him, she linked her arm with his.

Thaddeus waved his arms in a wide arc. "This is a special place, you know. At one time gods roamed the hills behind us. They lived close to humans, playing, fighting, loving. They were even called by names. I wish they were among us today."

Alex gazed at the three larger-than-life men who surrounded her and thought, *The descendants of those long-ago gods walk among us today.*

"Alex," Thaddeus said suddenly, "come with me. You must try some of our delicacies."

Sending Damon a smile, Alex picked up the train of her wedding dress with one hand, grabbed Zan with her other hand, and followed Thaddeus to a long table at the side of the terrace laded with fresh vegetables, cheeses, lamb, whole spit-roasted chickens with sauces on the side, fried baby squid, grilled octopus, huge chunks of bread, bowls of luscious black olives, trays of desserts that included pastries and custards, sugary cookies, and dishes of walnuts, almonds, and pistachios.

Thaddeus pointed toward a plate of grape leaves filled with meat, rice, tomato, and spices. "These are called dolmas, and I will not be happy unless you eat at least one."

Alex laughed. "I want to try everything."

"Wonderful! You have the spirit of a Greek woman!"

Beside her, Zan rolled his eyes and whispered, "You *are* feeling better. This is spicy stuff."

Thaddeus clapped his hands, attracting the attention of the crowd. "My friends, we will dance the *syrtaki*. Alex?"

She grinned, amused at how easily he had lost interest in the food. "If you don't mind, I think I will watch. And eat."

"Of course I don't mind," he said in his booming voice. "A bride needs her strength. What about you, Prince Al Iraj?"

"I'm going to help Alex eat."

Thaddeus's dark eyes sparkled with approval. "You must try the *melitzanes yemistes*. The lamb is superb. Eat. We will dance. And then we will all raise our glasses to the health of the bride and groom."

Already some of the villagers and wedding guests had linked together, arms around one another's shoulders, and were moving in unity to the music. Thaddeus rushed off to join the theme.

"That man makes me tired," Zan said dryly.

A knowing look sparked in Alex's eyes. "All right. We're alone. Say what you've been dying to say."

"Me?" He shook his head. "You're mistaken. I don't have anything to say."

"Zan."

"Well, I will say that you're a radiant bride, Alexandra. And an unorthodox one, I might add. What gave you the idea to use your pearls as a belt?" He nodded at where the iridescent necklace circled her waist, leaving the long ends to trail down the front of the ivory satin dress, reaching nearly to the hem.

"I thought they'd compliment the dress better this way."

His nod was very masculine, very Continental. "Quite a medieval look. I wish I could think this marriage was going to compliment you as well."

Her lips quirked with humor. "Smoothly done," she said, then turned serious. "I'm not a naive girl anymore, Zan. I know Damon doesn't love me and that I'm going to have to work very hard to make this marriage a success."

"The man is crazy for not loving you," Zan said flatly.

"It will work out. Be happy for me."

He patted her arm. "This marriage is what you want, and today is your day, my love. I am happy for you."

Alex spotted Damon across the terrace, talking with a couple he had introduced her to earlier. He was smiling and he actually looked relaxed. It was a good sign, she thought. Her gaze went around the party, finding a group of her friends who had flown in from Connecticut for the occasion. She waved at them, then continued her survey.

A man she hadn't met before slipped beneath the vine-covered trellised arch at the edge of the terrace. He was dressed too nicely to be one of the villagers, she thought, so he must be one of the wedding guests.

"Would you like something from the buffet?" Zan asked.

"I'll get it," she said absently.

Two more musicians had joined the group playing bazoukis. One added his clarinet to the song, the other, a dulcimer. Laughter vied with the music. The line of dancers dipped and swayed.

The man under the arch fixed his gaze on Damon, drew a gun, and took aim.

"*No!*" Alex screamed as she raced across the flagstones toward her husband.

Damon saw Emilio Delgado under the arch, but what had him frozen with fear was Alex, throwing herself into harm's way for him. He caught her to him just as the loud explosion of a gun discharging rent the air. And for one awful instant he believed Alex had been shot. Time splintered apart, giving him a bleak vision of life without her. Then reality reconstructed itself, and he saw Delgado fall forward, part of his head blown away.

Not knowing what was happening, Damon thrust Alex behind him, shielding her with his body.

Chaos descended on the taverna. All around them people were shouting and running. Graham raced to him, gun drawn.

"Did you kill Delgado?" Damon asked quickly.

Graham shook his head, his eyes scanning the area. "It wasn't any of our men either."

Damon cast a baffled look around, then suddenly stilled.

Kito was standing beneath a silver-leafed olive tree twenty yards away from the terrace. There was a faint smile on his lips and a smoking gun in his hand. As Damon watched, Kito thrust the pistol into the holster he wore beneath his beautifully tailored cream-colored sport coat.

Damon took an impulsive half step forward. But before he could utter a word, Kito turned on his heel and sauntered away. A moment later he was lost in the winding streets of the village.

Damon leaned over and pushed a button and the ceiling of his stateroom began to slide open. Then he settled back onto the big bed and drew Alex into his arms. She said she was all right, but she seemed unnaturally quiet.

The moment when he had thought her dead was still like a living nightmare in his mind. The whole incident had been all the more frightening because, beforehand, he hadn't experienced that peculiar, familiar need to be on the alert for the unexpected. The feeling had always stood him in good stead, but today the internal warning hadn't been there. His mind had been occupied with the wedding and his pending fatherhood; his senses had been dulled.

He would have to be more careful.

He drew Alex closer against him and pressed a kiss to her temple. "What are you thinking about?" he asked, afraid that he knew the answer.

"Kito."

"Try to put this afternoon out of your mind."

"How can I? You were nearly killed. Again." She gave a light, mirthless laugh. "That's twice I've seen someone nearly gun you down. I can't get used to it, Damon. I shouldn't have to."

"Shhh."

Alex shifted her head so that she could see Damon's face. "Why did Kito save your life? You told me he hated you."

"I've been asking myself the same question, but I have no answer. My understanding of Kito goes only so far and then stops."

"That you understand him at all is amazing."

"We share a common background, a personal history. We were raised as brothers, and time can't wipe that away."

Alex stayed quiet, hoping he would go on.

God, but he felt weary, he thought. The realization came as a surprise. Unfortunately this wasn't a weariness that would be alleviated by eight hours sleep. He leaned back against his pillow and closed his eyes. Holding Alex's slender body against him, he let the gentleness and warmth of the night air wash over him like a much-needed balm.

"My parents were teachers who looked beyond the facade of well-being the government expounded, and found intellectual and political repression. One day, when I was eight years old, they went off to participate in a demonstration they had helped organize. They kissed me good-bye and sent me to stay at Kito's house to wait for them. But about an hour after they left, I got a strange feeling and went after them."

He ran his hand up and down her arm. "I rounded a corner of a building and spotted them just as soldiers opened fire on their group. My mother and father were the first to go down. I cried out and tried to run to them, but someone held me back." His hand tightened on her arm. "I felt so helpless. So damned helpless. There was not a thing I could do. They were killed instantly."

Alex covered his hand with hers, and his grip slowly relaxed. She was aware, if he was not, of the importance of this moment. He was opening himself up to her, revealing a painful part of his past. And it gave her more hope for the two of them than the gold band on her finger.

"Kito had followed me. He took me home to his house. His mother, Cilka, put me into his bed. That night Kito lay beside me and for hours talked to me until I stopped crying. He was eight years old, too, and at that age might have resented having to share the affection of his mother and sister, not to mention food and clothing. But he didn't. Back then he was open and generous. There's never been anyone I was closer to.

"As we grew older, we became involved in an underground group whose purpose was to oppose the repressive regime. But with time the group turned more radical. Kito went along with their ideas and eventually emerged as their leader.

"I had seen what violence that was out of control could do. I left, slipping out of the country without telling anyone how I was getting out or where I was going, because I didn't want to get Kito or his family into trouble. A year later I received a letter from Cilka, and that was the last I heard from her. But as the years passed, it wasn't hard to keep up with Kito. I had only to open a newspaper or turn on the evening news. But I didn't actually hear from him until he gave you the cross."

"Why the cross?"

He hesitated. Certain things from his past still had the power to make him bleed. "Because it belonged to his sister, Chessy, and he knew that would get my attention as nothing else would."

"I still don't understand."

"One day I'll tell you all about it. But not now."

He fell quiet. He didn't know why he had told her about that day that his parents had been killed, that day that had sent his life spinning in a different direction. But somehow he felt better now that he had.

He felt Alex curl against him. Had there ever been another woman who was as silky-soft as she, he wondered. As open or as beautiful? He raised up on one elbow and brushed her hair away from her eyes. "I'm sorry your wedding day was ruined."

"You're alive," she said simply. "It wasn't ruined."

His original intention had been to hold and comfort her through the night, but now it seemed so natural to take her into his arms. To press his mouth to hers. To let his hand slide beneath her gown to the smooth warm flesh beneath. She was his wife this time. Surely there was no hurry or urgency. Surely he'd be able to leisurely savor the incredible experience of making love to her.

Her breast filled his hand. The gown was pushed higher.

Her nipple teased his tongue. The gown was discarded.

Now his mouth could roam. No pressure. No rush. Now his hands could caress, his fingers could stroke. But fires ignited quickly.

"Alex, how do you make me want you so?"

"I guess want makes want," she whispered. "I want you just as much." She gasped as his hand glided down her flat stomach, through the nest of auburn curls, and unerringly found the most sensitive spot on her body. "Oh, that feels good." Her fingers dug rows into his back as she arched to him.

"Tell me."

"You were my first lover. You'll be my only . . ."

"What?"

"Lover . . . husband."

He groaned and thrust his tongue into her mouth, seeking and tangling with her own tongue. At the same time, his fingers prodded and played, bringing nerves to life, dissolving her into a wild thing who moved against him without inhibition. She threaded her fingers through his hair and held him fast as heat mounted.

"Do you think I'll ever get enough of you?" he muttered, his mouth at her neck now, his fingers still touching her intimately, feeling the hot moist tightness, making himself insane with the thought of how soon he would drive into her.

Almost beyond talking, her words came out in gasps. "I . . . hope . . . not."

He took a gentle bite of her neck. Then licked. Then bit. Then sucked.

"Damon . . ."

He raised up over her and entered her. And like the stars above them, Damon and Alex burned hotter and brighter, continuing their lovemaking until the black velvet of the night disintegrated.

"Damon, wake up." Alex rubbed his back gently. "The sky is beginning to lighten and I want to go up on deck and see the sunrise."

"The sun rises every day, Alex." Half of his face

was buried in his pillow, and his words were muffled.

She laughed softly. "Come on. This will be the first full day that I am Mrs. Damon Barand, and I want to remember every minute of it."

He rolled over on his back and opened his eyes, curious as to what she was up to. She was sitting back on her heels, wearing a pair of shorts and a cropped top, and looking as fresh and lovely as a newly opened flower. "Aren't you tired? As I recall, we didn't get much rest during the night."

She shrugged. "I must still be running on the excitement of yesterday." She saw the dark look come over his face and hurried on. "I meant our wedding." She rested her hand over her stomach. "I feel like I've never had more energy, and something tells me this day is going to be fantastic. I consider it an omen. Our future will be bright, and my pregnancy will be easy, and our baby will be healthy and wonderful."

His face softened with good humor. "I hope so. All right. Give me a second to get some pants on."

Minutes later they stood at the bow of the *Ares* as it plowed through the Aegean heading west. Damon pulled Alex back against him and curved his arms around her waist. She'd been right. The day promised to be fantastic. Already glorious shades of lemon, pink, and blue were tinging the sky, and the sea was turning from purple to azure. Off the side of the *Ares*, dolphins played in the ship's wake, diving and tumbling through the water like frisky, fun-loving puppies.

New feelings of appreciation and contentment for what was around him coursed through him. Maybe it was as Alex had said, he thought. Maybe the dawning beauty of the day was a good omen.

"So, Mrs. Barand, what redecorating plans do you have?"

She threw a glance of surprise over her shoulder at him. "What?"

"Isn't that what all new brides do? Redecorate their husband's home?"

His question had been lightly asked, but, leaning her head back against his shoulder, she gave the matter serious consideration. There was no question that the *Ares* was a beautiful vessel. But for the first time she viewed it through the eyes of a woman who was going to be a mother in a few months, and she found herself disturbed by the idea of the ship as a full-time home. Instinctively, though, she knew that now wasn't the time to bring the matter up. She and Damon were too new with each other. Their marriage was like a house that had no foundation. That foundation had to be built stone by stone before their union would be strong and the two of them and their child could become the family she so desperately wanted them to be.

"Alex?" he prompted.

"I was just giving your question some thought. You don't seem to use your private salon very much. I think it would be a good idea to take some of your treasures out of the lounge and place them where more people could see and enjoy them, including you. The statue of Aphrodite would be lovely in your study. Or the painting of the moonlit scene. I could have it hung on the wall opposite your desk—"

"And I could feel the glow of the moon."

She twisted her head around, a smile of delight on her face. "You remembered."

He stared down at her, his expression soft. "Alexandra, would you make love with me?"

"Here?"

"You once said you'd make love with me anytime, anywhere."

"But someone might come out on the bridge and see us."

He walked them several steps backward until he came up against a waist-high storage console. "No one will see us if we're behind this," he said, and, with his arms around her, sank to the deck.

Eight

Damon's study door loomed before Alex. She raised her hand to knock, then quickly lowered it. *Dear Lord, how could she tell him?*

The past week had been the happiest she had ever known. Every day had seen new strength added to the bond between her and Damon that had begun with their wedding. The ease of their companionship seemed to grow with each hour, and, unbelievably, their lovemaking increased in intensity.

Now all that glorious closeness would turn to hate when she told him she wasn't pregnant. She ached as if she had received a tremendous blow to her body, and she had no idea how she was going to be able to get through the next few minutes.

She raised her hand again, then suddenly grasped the doorknob and entered the study.

"Alex." Damon's smile relieved the absorbed expression on his face. "I thought you were going to take a swim. Did you change your mind?"

Her eyes darted to Graham, then back to Damon. "I need to talk to you."

"We'll be finished in about an—"

"Now," she said, wrapping her arms around her waist, engulfed in misery. She looked at Graham. "I'm sorry, but I need to talk to Damon alone."

"Sure, no problem." Graham gathered up the papers around him and rolled to his feet. "Damon, just call me when you want to continue." Casting a concerned glance at Alex, he left the room.

When Damon moved to stand, she reacted violently.

"No!" She held out her hands, warding him off, convinced she would fall apart if he came close or touched her. "Don't get up."

He subsided back into his chair. "Alex, you're scaring me. What's wrong?"

She stiffened, bracing herself against the next wave of pain she knew was coming. "I don't quite know how to put this, so I'm just going to say it. I'm not pregnant."

"What in the hell are you talking about?"

"I—I just received a call from my doctor back in Connecticut. He's been trying to reach me for days now, but it took him a while to track me down. He wanted to tell me the results of my blood test. It seems, according to that test, that I'm not pregnant after all. The pregnancy test I took at the office gave a false positive."

Damon stared at her, thunderstruck. "How could something like that happen?"

The shock and disbelief on his face cut across her already-hurting heart like a newly honed blade. "It's entirely my fault. I wasn't feeling well when I went to him, and it turns out now I had the flu." She gave a hollow laugh and dropped her eyes from his. "At any rate, I wasn't thinking clearly, and I evidently gave him the wrong count of days from my last ovulation. He said it was a common mistake that a lot of women make. Unfortunately even if the count is off a week, the results can be false, and in my case I've never been regular anyway." She could feel herself faltering. "But, fortunately, at least I guess for us, he had drawn blood that same day, and . . . that test shows conclusively that I'm not pregnant."

She stared at her hands for a moment, then dared a look at him, and a cold feeling spread through her chest and tightened. His face was like a mask. "I'll move my things out of your stateroom immediately, of course. But I want you to know that I'm sorry. I wasn't trying to deceive you or trap you into marriage. I honestly thought I was pregnant or I never would have come to you. . . ." She trailed off, making a helpless gesture with her hands.

"You're going to move your things?" he asked quietly.

He didn't believe that she had never meant to deceive him, she thought, grief-stricken. "Yes, don't worry, I'll move them." Blindly she glanced around his study, thinking how pitiful the situation was. She had never really been pregnant, but, nevertheless, there was an emptiness in her. She had never really had Damon's love, but she had hoped she was earning it.

Now she had nothing.

Silence hung like a wall between them, becoming more solid as the seconds ticked by.

At last, realizing he was not going to say anything more, she turned and walked out of the room, shutting the door behind her.

Damon leaned his head against the back of his chair and shut his eyes.

Deep in the night, the *Ares* followed the moon's silver trail across the Aegean. Alex stood at the bow of the ship, wind tangling in her hair, sea spray misting her face. A week ago, on the morning after her wedding, she had stood at this very spot with Damon's arms around her. She'd felt such hope and happiness then, but she'd been foolish.

Damon had wanted her pearls so badly, he had kept her with him after the party in hopes that he could get her to sell them to him. When that didn't work, he had lost interest in her and sent her home. He had accepted her back into his life and married her only because of the baby.

He had returned the pearls to her on their wedding day. But, she asked herself, would she have ever seen the necklace again if she hadn't come back? Perhaps he planned to tell her that the pearls had been stolen while in transit from the jeweler. She would have believed him.

And there was one more thing. She raised her hand and touched the scar that ran along her jawline. Damon was a man who craved beauty around him. She should have known he would never be able to love a woman whose face was scarred.

A cloud drifted across the moon. She wrapped her arms around her body and raised her face to the wind. In a few hours they would be at Crete. Homer had written; "Out in the dark blue sea there lies a land called Crete, a rich and lovely land." But she wouldn't see any of Crete's wonders. If a charter couldn't be arranged, she planned to take the first flight available to anywhere. London. Athens. Rhodes. It didn't matter.

Cuts that were made quickly didn't hurt as much.

The moon broke free of the cloud and rayed silver light down on her . . . and on Damon, who stood behind her on the bridge, staring down at her.

The next morning Alex put her hand in Damon's, steadying herself as she stepped from the launch to the quay. When she was beside him, he pointed toward the Mercedes. "The car's waiting. I'll drop you off at the airport and then go on to my meeting."

Such ordinary conversation, she thought, her pain strangely dull and heavy now. Surely there should be a more meaningful exchange between a husband and wife who were about to part for good. But, perhaps, it was better this way. Words had such power to hurt. She avoided looking at him and, instead, concentrated on the surroundings.

A sea bird called overhead. A puppy scampered down the street, a small boy ran after him, laughing. An old man sat on a bench, reading a paper.

Then a wall of stillness descended.

The sea bird hung in the sky. The old man's hand paused in the act of turning a page of the paper. The puppy's yap and the child's happy laughter ceased.

Alex saw the bright burst of light before the sound registered on her senses.

Then the shock waves of the explosion threw her backward into Damon's arms.

Jerking her head in the direction of the roar, she saw the skeleton of the Mercedes outlined in flames.

The child picked up the puppy and hugged his pet to him. The old man stared, his mouth open with amazement. The sea bird flew away.

She tried to straighten, but Damon had her in a fiercely protective grip against his chest.

"Alex, Alex, are you all right?" His mouth was against her ear, his voice urgent.

"Yes, are you?"

Slowly he relaxed his hold on her and turned

her around. "Let me see. Are you sure, you're all right?"

She let out a gasp. Blood was streaming down the side of his face. "You're hurt!"

He raised a hand to his temple in surprise. "It's nothing. Just a scratch." His eyes alertly scanned the harbor and the dock area as he drew a white linen handkerchief from his pocket.

She took the handkerchief away from him and pressed it against the wound. "It must have been a fragment of metal from the explosion."

He grabbed her arm. "Come on. We need to get back to the ship immediately."

"But the airport."

Firmly, insistently, he guided her back onto the launch. "Alex, I don't know what's going on. But until I do, you're not leaving my sight."

A short time later Damon strode into the communications center. A tight-lipped Graham handed him a transcription of a call. It read: "See how vulnerable you and Alex are? Next time it will be Alex. First your suffering. Then your death."

Damon's face lost all color, and he tossed the note aside. "Graham, send out immediate notification to all our customers that we are no longer in the arms business."

"*What?* But we've already suspended shipment—"

"I'm not talking about just suspending shipments. I want *out* altogether."

"Damon, I can't believe I'm hearing this. Your wealth is diversified, but . . . what do you plan to do?"

"*Anything* but deal in violence and death."

"But—"

"Do it."

Graham picked up the note and quickly scanned it, thinking that he had missed something.

Damon went on speaking. "I got into this business because I thought I could make a difference in the world by controlling the violence," he said, his voice harsh with pain. "I was wrong. Violence can't be controlled."

Alex wasn't in her stateroom. Damon frowned and glanced toward the bed where one suitcase lay open. He crossed to the suitcase. A lacy camisole caught his eye. Idly he fingered the soft, feminine garment. Then he noticed an edge of the pale yellow dress she'd worn the afternoon he'd taken her ashore in Spain, and he reached for it. The summer frock weighed little more than a handful of air. He buried his face in the material and inhaled the scent of a Spanish sun and a flowered meadow.

Alex had come back to him only because she believed she'd gotten pregnant that afternoon. As soon as she discovered her error, she had moved out of his stateroom and made plans to leave him.

Years before, the process of getting rid of his child had killed Chessy, and her death had devastated him. From that point in time he had been careful that no woman would carry his baby. Alex had been the sole exception.

Dear God, why couldn't Alex have gotten pregnant that day.

He tossed the dress back into the suitcase, then pulled out the black velvet box that held her pearls, flipped open the lid, and stared at the magnificent rope.

When he had first seen them around Alex's neck, he had been obsessed with the idea of possessing the necklace for his very own. But in his excitement he had forgotten one very important thing: the admonition in the legend attached to the Pearls of Sharah.

The pearls were a gift of love, given and received freely, and they cannot be possessed. All who come in contact with the pearls will have their lives changed forever. And that change will be for the worse for those who try to possess the pearls.

The sight of Damon staring intently at her pearls made Alex pause in the doorway. *That damn necklace.* It was all he had ever wanted.

"Were you looking for me, Damon?" she asked, her voice sharp and hard to cover her hurt.

He snapped the lid closed and carefully placed the box back in the suitcase. "Yes. Where were you?"

"Out on the deck, walking, thinking." She pulled the large silk shawl she was wearing over her dress closer around her shoulders. She couldn't seem to get warm. "I can't get it out of my mind that another minute, and we would have been in that car."

He wanted to fold her against him and take away her shock. He stiffened his stance. "Try not to let what happened on the quay upset you. That bomb was only a demonstration. It was never meant to kill either of us."

She walked slowly into the room. "What do you mean?"

"Kito was showing me that he has my comings and goings timed down to the split second and that he can kill me anytime he chooses. It's all part of the mental-warfare game he's been playing."

"But how does he know so much about your schedule? You take great pains not to advertise where you'll be next."

"That's a good question." His lips tightened grimly. "And I think the answer lies with someone on board this ship."

"Someone who works for you is helping him?" she asked, growing colder.

His dark eyes were brooding as he looked at her. "The idea makes sense, doesn't it?"

She shivered, sending the shawl sliding off her shoulders.

Damon grabbed the silk triangle before it hit the floor, then carefully rearranged it around her. His hands lingered for a moment on her shoulders and then fell away.

"Thank you."

He stepped back. "I'm afraid you can't leave just yet."

"Oh?" She kept her tone neutral. "Why not?"

"I received a message from Kito in which he makes it very clear that you are in danger too."

"*Me?* That doesn't make sense. He could have done something to me that day on Corsica if he'd wanted to."

"I told you. He's been playing psychological warfare. But now his tactics are about to turn deadly."

"Oh, dear God."

He lightly touched her arm. "I don't want you worrying. I'm going to do everything in my power to keep you safe. That's why I want you on board with me."

He saw her hesitate. "Alex?"

"You're going to have to give me a minute. Since I've known you, there've been two attempts on your life." She laughed hollowly. "This may all seem part of a day's work to you, but the idea of someone out there wanting to harm me . . . or you . . . is frightening."

This time the instinct to reach for her was too powerful for him to repress, and he wrapped her in his arms. "I'm so sorry, Alex. All I can tell you is that I'll protect you with my life."

Just for a minute she allowed herself to go soft against him. *The cut of leaving wasn't to be quick after all,* she thought, but a few more days with Damon might be worth the pain. "I'll stay. For a while."

He breathed a sigh of relief. "Good."

She drew away and raised her hand to the thin, blood-caked ridge at his temple. "The bleeding has stopped, but the wound may leave a bad scar."

"Then we'll both have scars." He gave her a half smile. She touched her scar and dropped her eyes from his. He silently cursed himself. "Alex, I didn't mean—"

She moved to the dressing table. "It's all right. I've always known that scars on men are looked upon as interesting, while scars on women are looked upon as spoilers of their beauty."

"It's not that way at all."

Her laugh was brittle. "What are you talking about? You prize perfection so much, you wouldn't consider buying a vase with a flaw in it. Defective, I believe you said."

He recalled the conversation to which she was referring, and could summon no defense on his own behalf. On his way out of the room he stopped to run a finger over the Fabergé egg. "This ship is so perfectly detailed, you could almost imagine yourself standing by the main mast as you sailed toward new worlds, couldn't you?"

Just after midnight Alex opened the door to Benes's unexpected knock. He carried a silver tray. "I wondered if you might like some warm milk to help you sleep, Mrs. Barand."

"That's very thoughtful of you, Benes." She made a self-deprecating face. "I do seem to be having trouble sleeping tonight." She had donned her blue cotton nightgown but had been unable to bring herself to get into bed yet.

Benes advanced into the room, set the tray on a

table, and served the milk. "It is understandable, Mrs. Barand. You've had a troubling day."

"Yes." She sank into a chair, the glass of milk in hand. *A troubling day in many ways.* "Did you have to take Mr. Barand something to drink too?" she asked, unable to stop herself from fishing for information.

"Oh, Mr. Barand never has any trouble sleeping. But just to make sure, I knocked lightly on his door an hour ago. I received no answer. He is fast asleep."

Taking a sip of the warm, soothing milk, Alex's mind played with images of Damon asleep, alone in the big, oyster-satin-covered bed. And then she remembered the times she had slept beside him, wrapped in his arms. She wished with all her heart that she were with him now.

"Is the milk to your liking, Mrs. Barand?"

"What?" She jerked guiltily. "Oh, yes." She took several sips of the milk, then smiled back at him. "It's just what I needed. How did you know?"

He returned her smile. "As your steward, it is my job to anticipate."

"Well, you do your job very well."

"Thank you, Mrs. Barand. Now, if you don't mind, I will turn down your bed before I go."

"Certainly." Alex lounged back in the chair and began to drink the rest of the milk. Where would this all end, she wondered. In the space of a few weeks she had met, fallen in love with, and married an enigmatic man who sailed the seas on a fabulous yacht and who never let anyone get too close. He dealt with countries as if they were pieces on a chessboard, yet he rarely set foot on land, and once there, never stayed long.

And he never allowed his heart to be touched.

As soon as he found some way to get Kito under control, he would send her on her way. And then she'd have only memories by which to remember these strange, dangerous, wonderful weeks.

The room faded. The glass slipped from her fingers and fell onto the thick, rose-colored carpeting with hardly a sound.

Puzzled, she fought against the heaviness of her eyelids. But the room grew darker. And the last thing she saw before her eyes closed completely was Benes' smiling face above her.

At half past two in the morning Graham found Damon in the communications center.

"What are you doing still awake?"

"Kito's awake. I can feel him. The trouble is, I don't know where he is or what he's up to." He rounded on Graham. "Do you?"

Despite being startled by the suddenness of the question, Graham met Damon's eyes steadily. "If I knew, I'd tell you."

Damon held his gaze for a long minute, then turned away.

Graham watched Damon carefully. "Where are we headed?"

"Into the Ionian Sea."

"What's your plan."

"I'm waiting to see what Kito's next move is. I've never wanted him harmed, but he's threatened Alex now. That puts this game on a whole different level."

At half past three in the morning Kito double-checked his coordinates and adjusted his controls to bring his helicopter to a hover. He switched on the spotlight, scanned the bright light over the dark Aegean, then smiled with satisfaction as it picked out the life raft and the two people in it.

Nine

Damon burst into Graham's stateroom at six the next morning. "Alex is gone!"

Graham sat straight up in bed. "What?" And a heartbeat later, "In heaven's name, *how*? We've been at sea all night."

"One of the liferafts is gone and so is Benes." Damon rubbed the line between his brows. Fear stronger than any he had ever known had him in a stranglehold. He was functioning, giving orders, but all he could think of was Alex and whether she was safe.

As Graham slid out of bed and reached for his trousers, Damon said, "I've ordered the ship to turn around, retrace our route for several hours, then go into a searching pattern. The trouble is, I have no idea *when* Benes took her."

"Benes." Graham zipped up his pants. "Damon,

163

I did a thorough security check on him. He came out clean as a whistle."

"Looks like you slipped up."

"I'm sorry. I—"

"I don't want apologies," he said, his jaw set, his teeth clenched. "I want you to find where Kito is holding Alex."

"Well, sure, I'll go up to the bridge right away and—"

"No!" The thunder in Damon's voice made Graham take a step backward. "You will go up to the communications room and contact your bosses in the CIA."

Graham paled with shock. "How long have you known?"

"Right from the very first."

"But why didn't you say anything?"

"Why should I? Better the devil you know than the devil you don't. Like Benes, for instance." His angry words cut like glass shards.

"Damon, you're too powerful a man not to keep tabs on. With the force you wield, you can topple governments. We had to know at all times what you were doing."

Damon sliced a dismissive hand through the air. "I don't give a damn about that! Graham, I've never asked you to use your contacts before, because nothing's ever been this important. But I want the full strength of your organization behind this. I want Alex found before Kito—"

He broke off, and when he next looked at Graham, a very private hell burned brightly within his black eyes. "Graham, I love her. She's my life. I don't want to hear about red tape."

Graham nodded and started for the door. "Don't worry. I'll get all area operatives on it immediately."

Kito cradled Alex against his chest and held a glass of water to her lips. "Take a drink."

She pushed feebly at it. "Why? So you can drug me again?"

"No, so you can feel better." He put the glass to her mouth. "Come on."

Her head pounded; her mouth felt like cotton. She gave in and allowed some of the cool liquid to trickle into her mouth.

Kito gently lowered her head to the pillow. "There now. In a few minutes I'll give you some more."

Running a tongue over her dry lips, Alex gazed around her, trying to get her bearings. She was lying on a narrow bed in a small white room. A bright handwoven bedspread covered the bed. Sunlight poured through two steel-barred windows. An icon of the Virgin Mary hung on the wall beside her.

Kito observed her efforts. "We're on a small island in the Aegean. It's a quiet out-of-the way place I often use." He studied the room. "Damn," he said softly, "I'm so tired of it all."

"What?" she asked, confused.

"Nothing." He rubbed a hand over his face.

"Benes? I—"

"He's here. Wonderful, isn't he? I planted him

aboard the *Ares* eighteen months ago, and he's been invaluable. He even told me about Damon's obsession with your pearls. Leave it to Damon to get both you and the necklace."

A pain throbbed dully in her head. She shut her eyes. "What are you going to do with me?"

"Use you to lure Damon here."

Her eyes flew open. "What?"

"If you stay with him," Kito said softly as if he were talking to himself, "he'll destroy you, just like he destroyed Chessy."

"Chessy?"

"My sister." He made an impatient sound. "Didn't he tell you about her?"

"He mentioned her name."

His laugh was filled with contempt. "Mentioned her name. I suppose it *would* be embarrassing to tell your wife of the young girl you left broken-hearted and pregnant. She was so damned fright-ened, she wouldn't even come to me, her *brother*, for help."

It was the cracked sound of anguish in Kito's voice that brought Alex up and off the bed, but a wave of dizziness made her quickly sit back down.

"What in the hell do you think you're doing?" Kito asked angrily. "Give yourself more time. If you want anything, ask me."

The room slowly steadied. "I want to know if Damon knew that Chessy was pregnant."

"He says he didn't, but I don't believe him."

"I do," she said.

He smiled sadly. "Of course you do."

"No, you don't understand. I came back to Damon because I believed I was pregnant."

A troubled look came over his face. "You're pregnant?"

"No, I was mistaken, but Damon asked me to marry him on the strength of that belief."

He made an abrupt gesture with his hand. "It can't be as you say. Did you see the cross, Alex? Our father gave it to Chessy on her confirmation. She loved that cross and wore it all the time." His lips twisted unpleasantly. "I suppose she even had it on when she and Damon made their baby. Mama wanted to bury Chessy wearing her necklace, but I said no. I wanted to keep the cross so that I could always remember her and what Damon did to her. But most of all, I wanted to keep it so I could remember how much I hated him."

"If you really hated him, you wouldn't need a cross to remind you," she said with insight.

He grabbed her shoulders and shook her hard. "You don't know what you're talking about, Alex."

"Kito, you saved his life at our wedding reception."

He released her with a dismissive push. "Do you think I want anyone killing him but me?" His voice held pity at her lack of understanding. "The wheels are in motion, Alex. Cooperate with me, and you'll come out of this all right. Don't, and you'll die with your husband. Either way, it doesn't matter to me."

He walked to the door but paused and looked back. "Rest while you can, Alex. Soon you're going to need your strength."

Alex saw the door close after him and heard the click of a heavy bolt sliding into place. Weakly she lay back down. "Please, God," she whispered, a single tear sliding down her face, "don't let Damon find me. Keep him safe."

Hours later the door was flung open. "Get up, Alex. I've just received word that Damon is on his way here. He worked fast. Faster than I antici-pated." Suddenly his brow furrowed as if his thoughts were painful. "I wanted him to suffer longer, wondering whether you were dead or alive." He cut his eyes to her. "I'm sorry, Alex, but I'm going to have to change my plans. Who knows though? Maybe it will even work out better this way." He grabbed her arm and pulled her off the bed and to her feet.

Alex was relieved to find that her strength had returned and her head no longer throbbed. "Kito, think about what you're doing," she pleaded. "Damon was your friend. You were raised together as brothers. He left because of ideological differ-ences not because he loved you and Chessy any less."

Kito's mouth twisted into a snarl. "Damon shouldn't have left, Alex. Chessy and I needed him. The group needed him."

"Talk to him," she urged. "Try to come to some understanding."

"I said all I wanted to say the day of your wed-ding." He smiled as he saw the blank look on her face. "He didn't tell you, did he? Never mind. I'm sorry I have to do this to you, but just do what I tell you to, and soon this will all be over." He jerked her through a larger room and out the back door.

Dazzling sunshine and a strong, cool wind lashed at her. She flinched and blinked her eyes.

Kito drew her hard against his side. "The *meltemi*—the winds blow for us, Alex."

"Where are you taking me?" she asked anxiously.

"To the cliffs. Damon will find us, and when he does, I want his first sight of you to be memorable."

Damon stepped out the back door of the small white-washed house and gazed toward the cliffs. *Okay, Kito, the games are over.*

He shrugged out of his sport coat, dropped it on the ground, then reached to the back of his belt for his gun. He started up the hill, stopping minutes later when he saw Kito and Alex at the summit, outlined against a sharp blue sky. Kito had one arm crooked around Alex's neck, holding her against him so that her body partially shielded his. With his other arm he held a gun to her head.

Damon's heart slammed against his ribs, terrified for her. He stopped about ten feet away and raised his gun, taking the best sight he could on Kito. The problem was, he wouldn't be able to shoot without hitting Alex. "It's me you want, Kito." His voice was cool and completely steady.

"Let Alex go. She has nothing to do with what's between you and me. She's innocent."

"Chessy was innocent too, Damon, but it didn't matter, did it? She died anyway. This is my way of paying you back."

"My men have taken Benes and the others into custody. Give up. I have influence with many governments. Let me help you."

Kito laughed harshly. "It's gone too far, Damon. Don't you see? Not even you have enough influence to help me. Throw down your gun."

"No way."

Kito's smile was deadly. "Okay then, let's play." He hauled Alex closer to the rocky rim of the cliff. "How far down do you think it is, Damon?"

I'm about to die, Alex thought. The cold steel of Kito's gun barrel pressed bitingly against her temple. Horror gripped her mind. She fixed her gaze on Damon. He seemed so composed and dispassionate. Didn't anything ever touch him? His eyes were like hard black stone. She wanted them to soften and look at her. In this last moment before she died, she wanted to be able to believe that he loved her.

She gave a cry as Kito jerked her toward the edge. Kito's strident voice roared in her ears.

"Just one push and she'll go over. What do you think? Will she die instantly when she hits those rocks down there? Or do you think she'll lie there for a while, suffering in terrible pain?"

Damon slowly advanced, his gun held straight and steady. "If she goes over, you'll never see my reaction, because I'm going to kill you. Surrender and live, Kito. Kill her and die without ever seeing me suffer."

"You bastard!"

"Chessy's death made you crazy with grief, Kito, and you had to blame someone. I was the perfect person. But think. You used to know me better than anyone did. No matter how deep you've buried the knowledge, somewhere inside you you've got to know I would never have left if I had known."

A wavering light of uncertainty crossed Kito's face, then was gone. His arm around Alex's neck tightened. "She's scared out of her mind, just like Chessy must have been, Damon. How does that make you feel?"

Alex couldn't take anymore. She jerked away, stumbled, then heard the ominous cracking of rock. Before she could right herself, the ground shifted beneath her feet and began to break apart. Alex felt herself falling backward.

Kito dropped his gun and lunged frantically for her. His hand clamped around her wrist just as she slipped over.

Damon leapt forward, fell to the ground beside Kito, and looked over the edge. Alex was dangling in the air like a broken doll. He threw a helpless glance at Kito. "Can you pull her up?"

"My grip isn't that good," Kito muttered, his teeth clenched.

Lying on his stomach, Damon extended his arm down to her. "Grab my hand," he shouted.

Alex whimpered. Overmastering fear had her paralyzed, afraid to move, afraid to open her eyes.

"Alex," Damon called again. "Give me your hand."

"I can't."

"I don't know how much longer I can hold her," Kito said. Despite the cool wind, he was sweating and every muscle in his body was tensed with the effort of supporting her weight.

Damon gazed down at Alex. "Dammit, don't think about it. You've got to just do it!"

She flung up her free hand and hit rock. Flesh scraped off her palm, and she cried out in pain.

Kito gave a harsh grunt as her hand began to slide out of his.

Urgent panic scored Damon's voice. "Alex, you've got to open your eyes! Look up at me! Reach for my hand!"

She gritted her teeth and blocked everything from her mind but the need to obey Damon. She raised her hand again, and this time Damon grasped it. He and Kito worked together inching their bodies backward as they pulled their precious cargo slowly upward.

Finally Alex's upper body was angled over the precipice, and she swung a leg on top of the rock, gaining purchase.

As soon as he could, Damon grabbed her by the waist and rolled over and over. Safely away from the edge, he stopped, but didn't release her. He held her shaking body tightly to him. "It's all right, Alex. It's over now. You're safe."

Hot blinding tears scalded her eyes and choked her throat. She was safe, she thought, attempting to convince herself. She was in Damon's arms.

Kito came to his feet and stood looking down at them, his chest rising and falling with ragged, shuddering breaths. Then the rock beneath him began to give way. He yelled out.

Damon's head jerked up.

A look of terror crossed Kito's face as his eyes met his old friend's. *"Damon!"*

Damon started for him. But suddenly Kito was no longer there. Damon threw a quick glance at Alex. "Stay back!" He crawled to the cliff's newly formed edge and gazed down.

Kito lay lifeless on the rocks below, his arms and legs extended at unnatural angles like a puppet thrown down by a child who had tired of playing with his toy. A wave crashed over a boulder, misting him with its spray, and still he didn't move.

"Kito!" Damon shouted. The wind caught the sound of his anguish and pain and carried it out over the sea. But on the rocks below there was no answer, no movement. Damon sat back on his heels and dropped his head, feeling overwhelmingly defeated.

Despite his instructions to stay where she was, Alex crawled to him and put her hand on his shoulder. "Damon, don't blame yourself."

"I should have been able to save him."

"It wasn't your fault."

"Wasn't it?" he asked quietly.

"No. Stop thinking of him as that little boy you grew up with. He was an international criminal, and if he'd had his way, he would have killed us both."

He raised his head and looked at her. "I don't think he would have. In the end he helped me save you."

Damon's pain was harder for her to deal with than her own. "Time passes. Courses are set. No one can change them, and those who try get hurt. You did your best, that's all you can ask of yourself." She took his arm. "Come on now. We need to get away from the edge before it gives way again."

He gazed around, awareness dawning. "Dear God, I'm sorry. I wasn't thinking." He scrambled to his feet, pulling her up with him. When they were on safe ground, he drew her to him, held her wind-whipped hair to her head, and studied her. Scraps and cuts marred the pale skin of her face, neck, and arms, but to him she had never looked more beautiful.

He had nearly lost her forever. He wouldn't be able to bear it if she left him now. Somehow he had to convince her to stay. "You've been through a great deal," he said. "Let's go back to the ship so that you can rest. We'll talk later."

Ten

Alex paced the stateroom, unable to rest. She felt battered, but her condition was emotional, not physical. The experience on the cliff had been harrowing, but she knew that with time the horror of the day, along with the cuts and scrapes, would fade. What would never fade was the ache in her heart she'd always carry because Damon did not return her love.

She'd been on a roller coaster ever since she'd met him. Now she felt depleted, empty of everything vital. It was as if she'd been scraped raw on the inside, and there was nothing left.

And she'd come to a decision. Tired though she was, she could see no need to stay one more night on board the *Ares*. With the threat of violence over, Damon should have no objection to her leaving.

None at all.

She showered and changed into a sleeveless jade-green shift. At the last minute she added the pearls.

The sun had begun to lower in the sky and the *meltemi* no longer blew. From Damon's vantage point on the *Ares*'s topmost deck, the sea was like blue glass. Only a slight breeze stirred gently around him, breeze created by the *Ares* as it moved through the waters.

Damon could no longer see the island where his childhood friend had died, but a sadness remained in his heart. His parents, Kito, Chessy, Cilka—they were all gone now. All these years that chapter of his life had remained open and he hadn't even been aware of it. Now, though, the chapter was closed. A new life stretched before him. Whether that life would be empty or full depended on whether Alex would be with him.

When he heard her behind him, he turned in surprise. "Alex, what are you doing up here? I was hoping you'd be able to rest."

"I couldn't. How did it go with the authorities?"

He shrugged. "No problem. I didn't want you bothered, so I promised them a deposition from you."

"Fine." She hesitated, dreading the words to come yet wanting to get them out of the way. "Since I couldn't rest, I decided to go on into

Athens for the night. And then in the morning I'll get the first flight I can for New York."

He tensed, his pain more than he could have believed. "You want to leave tonight?"

She moistened her bottom lip with her tongue. "Yes, would you arrange for me a helicopter, please? Or would you rather I ask Graham to?"

"Alex, we need to talk."

She shook her head with despair. "I can't think about what. We spent a nice week or so together, we parted, and you would never have seen me again if I hadn't caught the flu and made a stupid mistake." She shrugged. "That about sums up the total of our relationship."

He stepped closer and put his hands on her arms. "No, you're wrong. There's much more. I love you, Alex."

A flame of hope flared, but she quickly extinguished it. She jerked away from him. "Since when, Damon? Since you first looked at me and saw my pearl necklace?"

His face tightened as he realized she was right to believe as she did. "I think I loved you almost from the first. I just didn't realize the love for what it was. I knew only that you kept me half mad with wanting you."

"Oh, I'll buy that. You desired me. But not enough to ask me to stay with you." Her laugh was a sound of pain. "I'll never forget that afternoon. We made love and an hour later I was in a helicopter, lifting off from this ship. It all happened so fast, I felt like I'd been run over by a truck."

His head jerked as if she'd slapped him. "I would have called you, you know. Sooner or later I wouldn't have been able to stand it without you, and I would have asked you to come back." His voice deepened with emotion. "I was miserable without you. I couldn't get through a night without dreaming of you or a day without wanting you."

"I don't believe you."

Helplessness surged through him. How could he get her to understand? "Alex, I wanted you constantly. In a short amount of time you had become vital to me. I was frightened because I didn't know what that sort of need meant." He grimaced. "Maybe the truth is, I didn't *want* to know. Your analysis of me that first night was right on the mark. Remember? A man who lives on a constantly moving yacht needs no one. I'd done a hell of a job convincing myself of that."

She felt as if something heavy were pressing on her chest. In her anger and hurt, she lashed out. "Stop it, Damon. This is futile. Why don't you just *once* before I leave this ship be honest with me. Tell me it was the pearls all along."

He never dropped his eyes from hers. "Yes, I wanted the pearls. At first."

She threw up a hand. "First, last, and always, Damon."

"Alex, I can't let you leave me."

"I'll tell you what. I'll make it easy for you to let

me leave. You can have the damned necklace."
She unwound the rope of pearls from her neck
and thrust them into Damon's hand. "There,
they're yours now."

Damon paled. "What are you doing?"

"I'm giving you what you want. I should have
admitted to myself sooner that it was the pearls
and not me you wanted. We both would have been
a lot happier if I had. Well," she amended bitterly,
"at least one of us would have been. You know,
it's ironic, but even Graham and Kito knew about
your obsession for the pearls."

Damon looked down at the pearls in his hand,
stunned. "Alex, you can't give me this necklace.
These pearls were your grandmother's."

"They mean nothing to me now."

"There's something I need to tell you about these
pearls, Alex. They're priceless."

"Good. Take them and be happy."

"No, you don't understand. These pearls are
not only priceless, they're very, very special. They're
called the Pearls of Sharah and are over twenty-
five hundred years old. They were given by a
Persian prince to a nomadic tribal princess named
Sharah. Through the centuries, a legend has been
attached to them and has grown until the pearls
seem to be endowed with almost mystical powers.
The pearls float mysteriously from person to person and time period to time period without explanation. Sometimes they will go for years without
surfacing, and then they just appear. Because

they were originally a gift of love, they cannot be used for evil, nor can they be possessed."

Her eyes teared, but she kept her shoulders erect. "Until now. Take them. Possess them in good health."

"I don't want them. I want you. I love you."

"No, you love the pearls. They're beautiful, because they're perfect. I'm not, remember?" She pulled back her hair, exposing her scar.

He groaned in anguish. "Alex, how can I explain this so you'll understand? Beauty was a hunger in me that wouldn't go away. It was like I had a bizarre kind of tapeworm in me that never got enough. I had a compulsion to acquire, to possess, but no matter how much I had, the treasures around me could never assuage my craving for beauty. I knew the history of each of my possessions: the artist, the period, the value. But I never felt anything when I looked at them. Not until you came into my life. You taught me what real beauty is, Alex."

She shook her head slowly, sadly. "It would be fatal to let myself believe you. I don't have any resources left within me to recover if you ask me to go away again."

"I won't. I love you."

Lord in heaven, she wanted to believe him, but she had been hurt too much. "Please, stop saying that!"

"What can I do to convince you?"

"There's nothing, absolutely *nothing* you can do."

He gazed down at the pearls in his hand, a thought forming slowly in his mind. The pearls nested in his palm and spilled through his fingers, shimmering with a luster that made them seem as alive as phosphorescent sea foam. "You don't want these pearls? You're giving them to me without condition?"

Her mouth twisted into a cynical line. "They're yours."

"Then I'll use them to prove to you that it's you I love." He drew back his arm and threw the pearls as far as he could.

They arced toward the sun, catching the light and shining with an unearthly beauty. For an instant they hung suspended in the air as if held by the unseen hand of a god. Then they dropped into the glistening azure sea and sank out of sight.

Alex stared at him, stunned.

"I love you," he said. "The most beautiful thing in my life was right before me all along, only I was too foolish to see it. *You.*"

"Damon . . ."

"There's something else. I'm retiring from the arms business. From this moment on I want to devote my life to you. We can live anywhere in the world you like, and we'll rename this ship and use it for holidays. I love you, Alex. Please, please don't leave me."

She went into his arms. "I love you too," she whispered, tears of joy coursing down her cheek.

Alex didn't know the story behind her grandmother's time with the pearls, but she did know the necklace had made Charlotte happy.

For a short period the necklace had been active in her own life. It had brought her together with Damon and proven, when nothing else could have, his love for her. The necklace had sealed her happiness.

For the moment the pearls had returned to the sea, their future uncertain. But, as for her and Damon, peace and happiness lay before them.

Mikos held a heavy stone to his chest as he swam deeper. He was exhausted. The other sponge divers were already topside, but he could no longer keep up with the young men and so he had been forced to make one last dive.

A pain gripped at Mikos's chest, reminding him of the deteriorated state of his lungs. This could very well be his last dive. The industry was changing; reforms, they called it. Too bad he wouldn't be around to benefit. He had spent his life harvesting sponges, diving in the age-old method of his ancestors, and he had little to show for it. How would he support his family when he could no longer dive? If only . . .

He peered intently through his face mask. Up ahead, in the sponge bed, something glimmered. *No.* Impossible. Nitrogen saturation was affecting his mind, he thought.

But then he saw the glimmering strand shift with the currents of the water; it moved across the sponges as if caressing the bosom of a woman. Curious, he swam toward it, his trident ready.

The magic of the fabulous Pearls of Sharah touches the lives of two more lovers in Fayrene Preston's next book
The Pearls of Sharah II,
RAINE'S STORY
April 1989
(on sale in March 1989)

THE EDITOR'S CORNER

With the very special holiday for romance lovers on the horizon, we're giving you a bouquet of half a dozen long-stemmed LOVESWEPTs next month. And we hope you'll think each of these "roses" is a perfect one of its kind.

We start with the romance of a pure white rose, **IT TAKES A THIEF**, LOVESWEPT #312, by Kay Hooper. As dreamily romantic as the old South in antebellum days, yet with all the panache of a modern-day romantic adventure film, Kay's love story is a delight . . . and yet another in her series that we've informally dubbed "Hagen Strikes Again!" Hero Dane Prescott is as enigmatic as he is handsome. A professional gambler, he would be perfectly at home on a riverboat plying the Mississippi a hundred years ago. But he is very much a man of today. And he has a vital secret . . . one he has shouldered for over a decade. Heroine Jennifer Chantry is a woman with a cause—to regain her family home, Belle Retour, lost by her father in a poker game. When these two meet, even the sultry southern air sizzles. You'll get reacquainted, too, in this story with some of the characters you've met before who revolve around that paunchy devil, Hagen—and you'll learn an intriguing thing or two about him. This fabulous story will also be published in hardcover, so be sure to ask your bookseller to reserve a collector's copy for you.

With the haunting sweetness and excitement of a blush-pink rose, **MS. FORTUNE'S MAN**, LOVESWEPT #313, by Barbara Boswell sweeps you into an emotion-packed universe. Nicole Fortune bounds into world-famous photographer Drake Austin's office and demands money for the support of his child. Drake is a rich and virile heartbreaker who is immediately stopped in his tracks by the breathtaking beauty and warmth of Nicole. The baby isn't his—and soon Nicole knows it—but he's not about to let the girl of his dreams get out of sight. That means he has

(continued)

to get involved with Nicole's eccentric family. Then the fun and the passion really begin. We think you'll find this romance a true charmer.

As dramatic as the symbol of passion, the red-red rose, **WILD HONEY,** LOVESWEPT #314, by Suzanne Forster will leave you breathless. Marc Renaud, a talented, dark, brooding film director, proves utterly irresistible to Sasha McCleod. And she proves equally irresistible to Marc, who knows he shouldn't let himself touch her. But they cannot deny what's between them, and, together, they create a fire storm of passion. Marc harbors a secret anguish; Sasha senses it, and it sears her soul, for she knows it prevents them from fully realizing their love for each other. With this romance of fierce, primitive, yet often tender emotion, we welcome Suzanne as a LOVESWEPT author and look forward to many more of her thrilling stories.

Vivid pink is the color of the rose Tami Hoag gives us in **MISMATCH,** LOVESWEPT #315. When volatile Bronwynn Prescott Pierson leaves her disloyal groom at the altar, she heads straight for Vermont and the dilapidated Victorian house that had meant a loving home to her in her childhood. The neighbor who finds her in distress just happens to be the most devastatingly handsome hunk of the decade, Wade Grayson. He's determined to protect her; she's determined to free him from his preoccupation with working night and day. Together they are enchanting ... then her "ex" shows up, followed by a pack of news hounds, and all heck breaks loose. As always, Tami gives us a whimsical, memorable romance full of humor and stormy passion.

Sparkling like a dew-covered yellow rose, **DIAMOND IN THE ROUGH,** LOVESWEPT #316, is full of the romantic comedy typical of Doris Parmett's stories. When Detective Dan Murdoch pushes his way into Millie Gordon's car and claims she's crashed his stakeout, she knows she's in trouble with the law ... or, rather, the

(continued)

lawman! Dan's just too virile, too attractive for his own good. When she's finally ready to admit that it's love she feels, Dan gets last-minute cold feet. Yet Millie insists he's a true hero and writes a book about him to prove it. In a surprising and thrilling climax, the lady gets her man . . . and you won't soon forget how she does it.

As delicate and exquisite as the quaint Talisman rose is Joan Elliott Pickart's contribution to your Valentine's Day reading pleasure. **RIDDLES AND RHYMES,** LOVE-SWEPT #317, gives us the return of wonderful Finn O'Casey and gives him a love story fit for his daring family. Finn discovers Liberty Shaw in the stacks of his favorite old bookstore . . . and he loses his heart in an instant. She is his potent fantasy come to life, and he can't believe his luck in finding her in one of his special haunts. But he is shocked to learn that the outrageous and loveable older woman who owned the bookstore has died, that Liberty is her niece, and that there is a mystery that puts his new lady in danger. In midsummer nights of sheer ecstasy Liberty and Finn find love . . . and danger. A rich and funny and exciting love story from Joan.

Have a wonderful holiday with your LOVESWEPT bouquet.

And do remember to drop us a line. We always enjoy hearing from you.

With every good wish,

Carolyn Nichols

Carolyn Nichols
Editor
LOVESWEPT
Bantam Books
666 Fifth Avenue
New York, NY 10103